THE MAGICAL REALMS

REALMS

Alfred's Story

H S Matthews

Table of Contents

Chapter 1...1

Chapter 2...6

Chapter 3...11

Chapter 4...15

Chapter 5...19

Chapter 6...23

Chapter 7...28

Chapter 8...33

Chapter 9...38

Chapter 10...42

Chapter 11...46

Chapter 12...50

Chapter 13...55

Chapter 14...59

Chapter 15...65

Chapter 16...70

Chapter 17...74

Chapter 18...79

Chapter 19...84

Chapter 20...89

Chapter 21...94

Chapter 22 | Beth..98

Chapter 23...104

Chapter 24...110

Chapter 25...116

Chapter 26...121

Chapter 27 | Almost twenty years later 126

Chapter 28...131

Chapter 29...136

Epilogue..140
About the Author...141
A message from the Author....................................142
Acknowledgement 143

To my family, my friends and readers, thank you X

.

Chapter 1

"Alfred, are you here?" Helen asked looking for her brother in his chambers. There was no answer and she presumed that he was in the meadows or woodlands looking for ingredients for his potions.

"Well my dear brother, if you are not here then I will just have to help myself," she continued with a chuckle.

Looking through Alfred's jars she soon found what she was looking for. Helen needed a potion for the crops, as they were not flourishing the way they should, she knew that Alfred would have something to help.

As she was leaving Alfred's room she heard a commotion outside, horses' hooves were pounding along the track towards their home. Helen was frightened, she was on her own as Harry and the boys had travelled into the town before sunrise to buy some provisions from the market.

Nervously Helen walked out into the yard, hiding the potion on the way. Luckily Harry had cloaked Alfred's chambers with an invisibility spell a long time ago as they were always wary of who might visit, she soon found out that today it was the King's guard filling the yard and they looked like they were on a mission.

"Are you the lady of the house?" one shouted at her.

"I am, can I help you?" Helen replied.

"The King has ordered a search of the area for anyone who is practising magic, you will let us look around the dwelling. Is there anyone else here?"

Helen told him that her husband and sons were at the market and would be back soon, she also told him that her brother was foraging in the woods for food for their dinner. He seemed to be satisfied and ordered his men to search their home.

"You will stay here while my men are inside," he ordered.

Helen nodded to him and opened the door, the guards barged past, almost knocking her over. She was not happy with their aggressiveness but held her tongue as she did not want to anger them.

As Helen stood outside listening to the guards in her home, she spotted Alfred coming out of the woods, Helen knew that he had seen the horses, but fortunately the guard in charge did not see him disappear back into the trees.

Alfred knew that he would only antagonise the guards if he went to help Helen, so he decided to keep his distance. He would only make himself known if Helen needed his help.

Minutes passed and Helen could hear their possessions being broken. Cups and plates clattered on the floor, it upset her, but it wasn't the first time it had happened. The guards callously destroyed things whilst they carried out searches in the area as if to deter any thoughts of resistance.

Finally the guards began to clear out of the family home, confirming to their commander that there was nothing found.

The Commander turned to Helen "My men are hungry; you would do well to provide us with some food and some water for the horses."

"I am afraid I can't offer you a meal, our crops have failed, and my husband is at the market to buy food for us, I can offer you water for your horses," she replied.

The guards were not happy and a couple of them went into the barn to check, they found nothing as the crops that the family did have were also cloaked, Helen and her husband Harry had learned long ago that the Kings guard would take everything they had and leave them struggling for food.

The horses were watered and soon the guards were leaving to torment the next family, she hoped that they were as prepared as her own was.

After a few minutes Alfred walked out of the woods towards Helen, he seemed calm, but she knew that he would be seething inside.

"Again? How many times is that this year Helen?" he commented.

"Quite a few, but at least you didn't upset them this time," she replied with a short laugh.

Alfred put his arm around his younger sister's shoulder and they both went back into the house to clean up the mess that the guards had left, and it was a lot of mess.

As they worked on cleaning the mess, they discussed ideas on what could be done to rectify the situation. Neither of them had any idea, it was foolish to try and oppose the King.

There was more noise outside. This time Helen smiled, she recognised her children's laughs immediately and went outside to greet them and her husband.

Harry seemed quite pleased and a little excited about something and Helen asked him straight away.

"Why the big daft grin on your face?"

"I have news, it could be wonderful for all of us. Where is Alfred?" Harry asked.

"He is inside; What is the news?" she asked impatiently.

Harry told Helen that he wanted to talk to her and Alfred together. Everyone went into the house, the boys were asked by their father to go and play outside, grudgingly they agreed and were soon out in the yard playing.

"Don't keep me waiting any longer," Helen said.

"While we were in the market there was a lot of talk about the King, it appears that he has found out that his physician was a sorcerer, he has been removed from the palace court and locked in a dungeon," he told them both.

"The poor man, when is his trial?" Alfred asked.

"I don't know, but the King is looking for a new physician, and I thought you should try and get the job," Harry replied.

"Why would Alfred want to work for that tyrant?!"

"We need somebody inside the palace to report what the King is planning and who better than a trusted physician?" Harry answered.

"It would take a long time for the King to trust a new physician if the last one has been caught practising magic, and why do you think he would have me as his new one?" Alfred said.

"Isn't it worth a try? We haven't had an opportunity like this before, it could be just what we need."

"Let me think about it, give me a day or two," Alfred said.

"We don't have a day or two for you to think, he wants applications by the end of today, you need to go to the castle and apply," Harry told Alfred.

Reluctantly Alfred agreed to apply, though he did not think he stood a chance. He asked Harry if he knew what he would have to do at the castle. Harry said he did not know what would be expected of him, only the King knew. Alfred was not impressed but said that he would get some things together and go there that day.

Chapter 2

Alfred packed a few of his herbs and plants, just the sort of thing used for medicine in case he had to show what he could do. He was nervous and a little annoyed that he had been put in this position, but he knew that they needed to do something to help save the magical population of the realm.

"Do you want me to come with you Alfred?" Harry asked.

Alfred told him to stay with Helen and the boys just in case the Kings guard came back again.

"I will be back late tomorrow. Well, I hope I will," he told Harry.

Helen and Harry both wished Alfred good luck and told him to be careful while he was travelling and even more so while he was at the castle. Both would have dangers and they all knew that.

Alfred set off through the woodlands that surrounded their home, it would be a long journey and it would take him until late afternoon to arrive at the castle.

The woodlands were centuries old and full of very ancient and gnarled trees, there were also wonderful plants that were found nowhere else in the realm, so as he was walking, he collected a few for his collection.

After a couple of hours walking through the woods, he arrived at the bottom of the mountain range he would need to travel through, it was filled with hazards, and he would have to watch his step as he went. There were rocks to walk on and streams to cross, he didn't want to injure himself. Alfred had not been in the mountains for a long time, he avoided them because of the stories of the dragons attacking people.

Long ago the King had waged war on the dragons, their numbers were decreasing by the month. Alfred felt sorry for them, but he didn't know how he could help apart from getting into the King's court and spy.

Once Alfred found the pathway around the base of the mountains the second part of his journey was short in comparison to the woodlands. Soon out of the mountains, Alfred was in stunning meadowland filled with the wonderful scent of wildflowers, again he collected plants along the way.

The meadowland was very open and there would be nowhere to hide if he was attacked, he kept his fingers crossed that there was nobody or nothing about.

Alfred was lucky, within an hour he was at the castle gates. He was tired from the journey and wondered what would be expected from him by the King.

Alfred approached a guard and told him that he was there to apply for the physician's position with the King, he was shown to a great hall where a few others were waiting. The hall was decorated with huge tapestries, each depicting a past Kings and Queens. He looked around and saw the one of this King. There was no tapestry of a Queen. Alfred thought that the King was too vain to share his throne. It was rumoured that this was the reason why the King's wife had not been made a Queen on the day of their marriage. Alfred wondered if she ever would be.

One by one the people waiting to see the King were taken into another room, none of them returned to the hall and so

Alfred presumed that they were seen by the King and then left the castle.

As Alfred was waiting, he studied the others. Their ages varied from young to old, and very old. Alfred was in the old category; he had been alive for many years. Alfred was in his thirties when his sister was born to his father's second wife.

Alfred was suddenly torn from his thoughts by a commotion in the hall. A young maid had come running in and was screaming that the baby prince was ill, she was shouting for help.

"What is the matter with him?" One of the others asked.

"He is dying!" she screamed.

The King came out of his room and asked what the noise was about, he was angry at the disruption until he found out that his only child was seriously ill.

The King rushed out of the hall with the maid, followed by a few of the applicants for the physician's role, including Alfred. It was not long before they were all at the door of the nursery, one of the prince's maids was cradling the baby in her arms when they opened the door, tears streaming down her face.

"Please help me! He's dying!" she cried.

"Whoever saves my son will be my new physician," the King told them.

There were four of them, including Alfred and they all entered the room. With the King's permission, the baby was placed on a table in the middle of the room. With solemn expressions, each applicant stepped forward to examine him.

After a few minutes each of them suggested a treatment, but Alfred knew straight away that none of them would work. He recognised straight away by the look of the child that he had been enchanted by magic. Alfred's problem was that he could not tell the King that, instead he would have to come up with a treatment to remove the enchantment without it looking like he was using magic himself.

"Sire, I have seen this before, it is a very unusual ailment, I can cure him, but I need to collect some specific herbs to make a medicine for the baby, will you let me try?" he said to the King.

"Whatever you need," the King replied. The other physicians seemed very put out by Alfred and they were soon escorted from the room by the guards.

"Do you have a kitchen garden?" he asked.

Alfred was told that they did, and he was shown the way by the maid. Once in the garden he collected an assortment of herbs. Alfred knew that he needed to make it look like he was making the medicine from the ingredients he found there, but he would also be using some of the rare plants he already had with him, and one of the hidden potions.

The prince had been enchanted with a spell that would leave him hovering between life and death if Alfred could not remove it. He had seen this before and knew exactly who had cast the enchantment. Once he cured the baby, he would seek her out.

"Do you have a room where I can make the medicine?" he asked the King once he had collected everything.

"You can use the physicians' rooms, there should be all of the equipment you need there," he was told.

One of the guards escorted Alfred to the room, when he entered, he saw more equipment than he had ever seen before.

Alfred soon found what he needed and got started on making the potion.

Chapter 3

Alfred soon found his way around the rooms, he gathered the equipment together that he needed to make a potion for the baby, it would take a little while and he knew that his time was limited. The enchantment would soon take the soul of the baby and once that happened there would be no way to save him.

Alfred sorted the ingredients he needed, chopped some and ground others, soon they were all boiling on a flame, steam rising from the liquid.

The guard stood by the door watching Alfred intently, it made him very uncomfortable, he needed to find a way to get rid of him so that he could add the final ingredient, a touch of magic.

"Excuse me, do you know if it is possible to get some orange tipped honey blossom here in the castle?" Alfred asked the guard.

"I don't know, but I can see if anyone knows," he replied.

"I need some urgently, could you find out now?"

"I am not allowed to leave you alone; can it wait until my replacement arrives in an hour or so?" the guard asked.

Alfred explained that without the orange tipped honey blossom it was possible that the medicine would not work on the baby, he told the guard that it was life or death.

"Okay, I will see if anyone knows where we can find some."

The guard left the room in search of the ingredient that Alfred had asked for. As soon as the door closed, Alfred reached deep into his coat and searched for the magic ingredient he needed.

After a bit of rummaging about Alfred found the small bottle containing the weeping dragon tears, he knew that this was what was needed to finish his potion.

Alfred dropped three tears into the brew that was now cooling on the table. As the third drop fell into the liquid it turned a bright yellow and a puff of smoke rose from the liquid and quickly dissipated. The potion was ready.

The door opened and the guard entered the room, he handed Alfred the orange tipped honey blossom. Alfred thanked him and chopped some into very fine pieces, he pretended to drop them in the potion, the guard was watching him closely.

Alfred swirled the bottle around so that the guard thought he was mixing the medicine.

"Can you take me back to the King please, the medicine is ready?" he asked the guard. He nodded, and Alfred followed him back to the baby's nursery.

"Have you got the medicine?" he was asked as soon as he walked into the nursery.

Alfred told the King that he did, and he asked to see the baby. The baby was pale and lifeless, and Alfred wondered if he was too late, but he wouldn't know for sure until he administered the medicine.

"When will we know if the medicine has worked?" the King asked.

"It will be immediate my Lord, I just hope that I have made it in time for the baby prince."

The King handed his son to Alfred. Once the baby was in his arms Alfred dripped two drops of the potion into his open mouth. As Alfred predicted the baby opened his eyes, he smiled up at Alfred. It had worked, he had succeeded in removing the enchantment.

The King and his advisers were overjoyed, the baby prince was sitting up and smiling at everyone around him, Alfred felt a strong bond to the child immediately, he knew that he was where he was supposed to be in that moment.

"What is your name?" the King asked.

"My name is Alfred your Majesty."

"How did you know what was wrong with my son?"

"Sire, I have seen this before in other babies from my village, I am just glad I was able to help," he replied.

Alfred was very careful not to let the King know that it was a magical enchantment, it would not take much for a full-scale hunt to be ordered to find out who did it. Alfred already knew, there was only one sorceress that could perform that enchantment and Alfred would not give her life to the King. Alfred still loved her, and he knew he always would.

"Well Alfred, would you take the position of royal physician?" the King offered.

"I would be honoured your Majesty," he replied.

Alfred was pleased that his mission had been accomplished but felt that it had been a little bit too easy, it was a very big coincidence that there was a major medical emergency with the prince just as he was in the castle. Alfred's mind wondered to thoughts of Kyra, was she involved in this? Did she make sure that Alfred had secured the position within the King's court?

The King ordered one his guards to show Alfred around the castle and then to his rooms. Alfred had a tour, and the guard gave him some advice on how to deal with the King, from what he was told the King did live up to his reputation.

The next few days involved Alfred getting to know the staff in the castle, as well as finding his way around. He got lost several times but was slowly getting used to the vastness of the castle.

Chapter 4

Life trundled on in the castle, Alfred had been asked to treat various servants in the castle for minor ailments, along with cuts and grazes, nothing too taxing.

Each morning he would start the day with a visit to the baby prince to check on him. He became very attached to young James; he was a cheerful and easy-going child with a smile that melted Alfred's heart. On each of his visits he hoped to meet the boy's mother, but she was never there. One morning he asked the maid that took care of James where she was.

"We aren't allowed to utter her name, let alone talk about what happened to her," the maid told him.

Alfred was puzzled but asked her again, explaining to her that he needed to be aware of anything he might do or say that could anger the King.

"I can't really tell you much; not long after James was born, she became ill and took to her bed but after a few days she seemed to be getting better and started to visit the baby. I was her maid and looked after James while she was getting better, the King arranged for another maid to take care of her. I had not met her before; she was from outside the castle. We were all glad she was getting better, she was loved by everyone here as she had such a gentle demeanour, she was so kind to us," she explained.

Alfred listened without interrupting as the maid continued.

"Anyway, we all thought she was getting better and back to normal when there was news one morning to say that she had died during the night, we couldn't believe it, honestly we still don't. Nobody saw her body and the King told us all that she had been taken back to her home village and buried there. Nobody was able to pay their respects and suddenly it was if she was never here. It was all very odd. The maid that was looking after her disappeared immediately with no explanation from anyone."

Alfred asked her a couple more questions, but she couldn't really answer them, she had been with James most of the time so didn't see much of what was happening. He thought it odd though that she had died when she seemed to be getting better. Alfred asked the maid if there was anyone who he could ask for more detail. The maid explained that nobody dared to talk about it, she said that the King had banned them all from discussing it; Alfred could tell that she feared the King and didn't want to talk anymore, so he thanked her and left her with James.

The days passed, Alfred listened intently to conversations in the castle, he was hoping to find out more about James' mother, but nobody was discussing her at all, he thought that most of the gossip about it would have happened immediately after her death and as it had been a few months the subject had been forgotten.

It was market day and Alfred was due to meet Helen, she was coming into the town to see him and buy provisions for the farm, he was looking forward to it. He left his room and walked out of the castle towards the market square. As he approached, he could see her sat waiting for him, smiling to himself, he realised that had missed her more than he expected.

"Helen, you look so well," he said as he hugged her tight.

"So do you Alfred, although maybe a little troubled," she replied.

"Let's go somewhere quiet."

Helen nodded and Alfred guided her to a quiet area at the edge of the market, where they sat down, Alfred told her all about his first few days at the castle. Helen listened about how he had healed the baby prince, about his suspicions that the illness could have been an enchantment and his conversation with the maid.

"Helen, I think that Kyra is involved in this, I have an uneasy feeling, the prince could be in serious danger."

"Kyra was captured and executed by the King a long time ago Alfred, she can't be the one that did this, you saw her die didn't you?"

"I did, but I am doubting it, we both know she was very powerful, she could have escaped, couldn't she?" he replied.

"Alfred, I was very young and don't remember too much about her, apart from how much you loved her. I know you were devastated when you lost her, but I don't know how she would have got away from the executioner. Alfred she was killed in front of a huge crowd, wasn't she?"

Alfred nodded, there were tears pricking his eyes, he knew that Kyra had been responsible for a lot of attacks on the King with her magic, he missed her every day.

"How can you explain the enchantment? Only she could have done that to the baby?" he asked.

"I don't know Alfred, let me see if there are any whispers in the villages, somebody might know something."

Alfred accompanied Helen around the market stalls and helped her with the provisions, soon it was time for her to start travelling home and time to say goodbye for a little while. Once the cart was loaded Alfred hugged his sister, he missed living with her, he hoped it wouldn't be long until he was back home again.

"Bye Alfred, I will see you soon. Next time I will bring the boys to see you, I know they miss their uncle."

"Give them my love, see you soon Helen," he replied.

Alfred watched his sister travelling out of the market and back towards home, in that moment he had a bad feeling, and he didn't know why.

"Alfred, the King wants you," he heard shouted.

"I am on my way."

Chapter 5

The days soon became weeks, the weeks soon became a few months, Alfred worked away at his new job slowly gaining the trust of the people in the castle and more importantly the King. He kept his head down and his magic hidden, so that everyone who visited with an ailment truly believed that he was a physician and not a sorcerer.

Kyra was on Alfred's mind quite a lot, he had not managed to figure out how the prince was enchanted with her magic or why they had chosen the baby. Alfred investigated the enchantment a bit more. It appeared that the spell was life threatening at first glance, but the more he researched it, the more it became clear that it was only a temporary spell, just enough to instil fear in those around the victim. Prince James would have recovered within a few days with no lasting effects from it, so what was the goal? What had the person who cast the enchantment achieved?

Alfred decided that if he wanted answers, he would need to travel to Kyra's home village and see if there was anyone else there that could do the same magic, maybe a sister, aunt or cousin. Alfred decided that he would ask the King for a few days off to go, and he hoped that he would say yes.

At first the King was a bit annoyed that Alfred had asked for some time off, but after reassuring him that he would only be a few days he relented.

It didn't take long to get a few things together and soon Alfred was walking out of the castle and back into the meadowlands that he had walked through the day that he arrived. It had been a long time since he had visited the village that Kyra had come from, he wasn't sure if anyone there would be able to answer any of his questions, but he didn't have anywhere else to start.

The journey to the village would take a full day. It was far enough from the castle for the King to be unaware of the magic but close enough that the villagers could keep themselves informed about what the King was planning. The journey would not be too difficult, as this time Alfred was on horseback and the terrain was mainly tracks through woodland and meadows, no mountain trails to navigate.

The sun was shining, the days were now warm. Summer had arrived and the meadowlands were in full bloom, filled with bees, insects and songbirds. It made Alfred happy and content to see the natural world in all its splendour and of course he gathered plants on his way, because you can never have too much in your store for magic potions.

The journey was mostly quiet; he met a few people along the way who were on their way to the castle for one reason or another. Alfred stopped along the way for some lunch and sat under a very old tree in the shade, it thought it must be over a hundred years old, it was huge and gnarled and could probably tell a few stories.

As he was sitting in the shade of the tree a shadow blocked out the dappled sunlight that was touching Alfred's face causing him to look up. He saw nothing immediately but kept looking. When it happened a second time, he saw what was causing it. It had been a long time since he last saw a dragon in flight as they never usually came anywhere near the castle. Alfred was curious why it was flying so close today.

Alfred stood up and stepped out from under the tree and into a clearing, sure that the dragon would spot him. As soon as he did, he began his descent until he stood in front of Alfred. As soon as he saw the dragon properly, Alfred smiled, and knew that there was no reason for him to be afraid.

"Agra, my old friend, it's been a long time. What are you doing this close to the castle?" he asked.

"I was close by, and I felt your presence and wanted to say hello. As you said it has been a long time," he replied.

"Where are you travelling to? Would you like a lift?"

"I am on my way to Kyra's village and yes a lift would be wonderful, I will just tether my horse and make sure he is near water while I am gone," Alfred told him.

Within a few minutes Alfred had climbed onto Agra's back and they were flying towards the village, away from the woods. When Alfred told Agra why he was going to the village, Agra agreed that to get any answers that was the place to start.

Agra then told Alfred about the losses the dragons had suffered, he told him that the last magical dragon Tora had disappeared and assumed killed by the King. It saddened Alfred to hear that, Tora had been a wonderful dragon and a good friend to the magical folk in the realm.

"Are the rest of you safe? Have you found somewhere to hide away from the King?"

"We have indeed; it is through a cave system and inaccessible to the King and his guards."

Alfred was happy to hear that, dragons were a majestic and wonderful creature with a huge capacity to empathise with the magical folk in the realm, they had all lost so much since the

King came to power. He hoped that one day there would be peace and that the dragons would be safe once again.

It wasn't long before they arrived just outside the village. Agra landed on the outskirts and Alfred climbed down. Once they had said their goodbyes, each of them wished the other good luck and to stay safe, they parted ways. Alfred walked into the village that he had once known as home when Kyra was alive.

As he walked into the village centre a loud bellowing voice shouted at him.

"And what do you think you are doing here???"

Alfred recognised the voice immediately and turned towards it, he saw his old friend and adversary Faren stood with his hands on his hips, and a smile on his face.

"Faren, how are you? You look well," Alfred commented.

"I am well Alfred, it's wonderful to see you, it has been a long time my friend."

Alfred had not visited the village since he came back to tell them that Kyra had died, he felt awful that he had not come sooner. Both men had aged a lot since they last saw each other, each had greying hair and wrinkles to show their years.

"Come my friend, let's get some ale at the tavern and catch up, shall we?" he said pointing at the building.

Chapter 6

The two men walked towards the tavern, chatting but not really talking, Alfred was wondering how to bring up the subject of Kyra with her brother, while Faren wondered how he would tell Alfred the news he had found out a few years ago.

Faren led Alfred to a quiet table in the corner of the tavern away from everyone, he could sense that Alfred was feeling as troubled as he was. Their close bond and usual ease in conversation with one another, now replaced by a strained and uneasy silence. This seemed more than just the passage of time since their last meeting, neither man knew exactly where to start when it came to discussing Kyra.

Eventually Alfred decided to get straight to the point and began to explain to Faren what had happened with the prince, his friend listened to all that he said and at Alfred's puzzlement at the use of Kyra's magic. As Faren listened he realised that he knew exactly why her magic was evident, but how was he to tell Alfred? There was only one way, and it was directly.

"Alfred, this is going to be difficult for you and maybe I should have told you long ago, but we never saw you, you distanced yourself from us when Kyra died. I should have tried harder, I am sorry, but you are here now, and it is time for you to know," he began.

"I was to blame too, I could have come and visited you, but it was just so hard to believe that she was gone, I just couldn't face anyone, and each day it got harder to pluck up the courage to visit," he told Faren.

"Alfred, a few years ago a young woman visited the village, she looked so familiar, there was just something about her," he began.

"The young woman asked for me in the village, I met her here in the tavern. She was quiet to start with, but eventually she told me something that surprised me; Alfred, she told me that Kyra was her mother, she was my niece," he continued.

Alfred was shocked, he didn't know that Kyra had a child, all sorts of questions were going around in his head.

When he finally found his voice, he asked her name.

"It was Dalfre," he replied.

Alfred was stunned to hear that the wife of the King, the mother of the prince was Faren's niece. He needed to find out more.

"What happened to her?" he asked.

Faren told Alfred that she stayed with them for a long while and got to know the family, but one day she was out in the woods looking for wild mushrooms for lunch when she disappeared, nobody knew where she went.

"We searched for her, but there were no clues to where she had gone, there was no sign of a struggle, we just hoped that she was safe. One day we heard that the King was getting married and wanted her family to attend. We were summoned to the castle and watched her marry the man who was destroying magic."

He went on to tell Alfred that Dalfre had magic like her mother and that she must have kept it hidden from the King, he told him that he had heard that once they were married it did not take long for her to become pregnant with the prince, but as soon as she gave birth, the family were informed that she had died.

"It was as if the King just wanted an heir. He took her from us, and we never saw her once they were married."

"Who was her father Faren?" Alfred asked.

"Do you need to ask that Alfred?" he replied.

"Yes, yes, I do, and when did they meet? Was it when I was away protecting the elders? I know I was away for a while, but I thought she loved me and would wait for my return." Alfred was hurt that Kyra may have been with another.

"Alfred, she was never with anyone else, we believe that Dalfre was your daughter and for some reason Kyra gave her away to another family to raise. We don't know why; we hadn't known that she was pregnant. Kyra went away for a while; she told us that she was going to help you. When she came back, she said that she never found you. Not long after that she was captured by the Kings guard for using magic, and that was when we all saw her again, on the day of her execution. Alfred she never got the chance to tell you about your daughter."

Alfred didn't know what to say. He had just found out that he had a daughter, one that he will never be able to meet because she was already gone. How was he supposed to deal with that he thought?

"I need to find out where she is buried, I must seek out the place she lays so that I can talk to her, I must explain that I never knew about her," he told Faren.

Faren understood that Alfred needed to speak to her, even if she couldn't hear him. He needed to say goodbye to the daughter he had never known.

"I will go back to the castle tomorrow and see if I can find out where she is buried, I will send word to you so that you know as well once I find out," he said.

"Come and stay with me tonight, we have a spare bed, the family will be happy to see you."

Alfred declined and said that he needed some time to digest what he had found out. He told Faren that he would get a room in the tavern but that he would see him before he left in the morning. Faren understood and told him that he and Saria would have a hearty breakfast ready for him the next day.

The men said goodnight to each other after Alfred had sorted out a room for the night.

"Thank you for the information, Faren, it will take a while for me to take in the news, to be honest it has knocked the wind out of me. I will see you tomorrow."

Alfred went up to the room that he was given in the tavern, he lay on his bed and sobbed. How could he not know he had a daughter? Why didn't Kyra tell him? What was her life like? Did she know that he was her father? There were so many questions going around in his head, he didn't know if he would ever forgive Kyra for giving their daughter away.

Sleep eluded Alfred for a long time, but eventually, as the darkness surrounded him, he drifted into a restless slumber. His dreams were filled of a daughter he never knew, and never could know.

When he woke the next morning, his head was filled with more questions that nobody would be able to answer, and he didn't know how he would deal with that. One thing he did know was that if everything he had learned proved to be true, he was the grandfather of Prince James. That wonderful child whom he adored and that made him both happy and sad at the same time.

He knew in that moment that James would never know who he was.

Chapter 7

Alfred left the tavern early. He walked to Faren's house and knocked on the door, his old friend opened it.

"Morning Alfred, was the tavern okay for you last night? Did you get some rest?"

Alfred told him that the room was comfortable, but he had trouble sleeping.

It was obvious to Saria that neither man knew how to act after last night's revelations. Each man's guilt written on their faces. She decided to take matters into her own hands.

"Are you ready for a breakfast feast Alfred? I've been up since sunrise."

Alfred remembered what a wonderful cook Saria was, he could smell the wonderful aroma's coming from their stove. His mouth was watering in anticipation.

"I been so long, it is wonderful to see you," Saria said as she put her arms around Alfred and hugged him tight.

Alfred realised in that moment what he had missed out on, he hugged Saria back and told her that he was sorry it had taken him so long to visit, he regretted not coming sooner. The three friends sat at a big wooden table in front of the stove, it was filled with so much food that Alfred did not know what to start with. There was bacon, sausages, eggs, wild mushroom, bread, hot scones and a big pot of coffee, all were sending out amazing aromas into the room.

To Saria's relief, both men seemed to relax at the sight of the food. The situation that had arisen between them could not possibly be resolved over one meal, she hoped that this would at least begin the healing.

"There is so much food here Saria, are you expecting an army to descend?" Alfred asked.

"No, just you and the rest of the family, they will be here very soon," she answered.

As she was finishing her sentence the door opened and in walked their two children and their families. Soon there were twelve of them sat around the table, there were the grown children and grandchildren and all welcomed Alfred. Amongst the laughter and chatter Alfred found himself feeling guilty for not seeing the children grow into adults, he had missed out on so much. A couple of hours soon passed, with lots of news and stories of the past shared.

Once breakfast was eaten and the kitchen cleaned away Alfred thanked Faren and his family for their hospitality and promised that he would visit again very soon, and he believed that he would. It was hard to say goodbye, but he was eager to get back to the castle to find out all he could about Dalfre and where she was buried. Alfred hugged his friends and said goodbye to them all.

The walk out of the village was difficult for Alfred, he imagined Kyra and Dalfre here, he felt lost. It wasn't long before he was back out into the countryside and the long walk back to his horse. He almost wished that he had not taken Agra up on his offer of flying him here, but the long walk would do him good as it would give him time to think.

It was dusk before Alfred got back to the woods where his horse was tethered, exactly where he left it. He decided to camp in the woods for the night and carry on his journey in the morning. Saria had sent him on his way with some of her wonderful food, so he gathered some ferns and made himself a comfortable bed to sleep and lit a fire to keep warm. Once he had eaten, he settled for the night and slept, he was exhausted, so sleep came quickly.

The sun was quite high in the sky when Alfred woke, he was startled to see a woman sat by his fire, which was surprisingly still burning.

"Who are you?" he asked.

The woman didn't say anything, Alfred studied her - she was a striking woman, about the same age as him he thought, maybe slightly younger. She had the clearest and deepest blue eyes he had ever seen. He found himself felling uncomfortable, until she finally spoke.

"My name is Elizabeth, but you can call me Beth.'

"And what are you doing here? What do you want?"

Beth took a deep breath and began to speak.

"I know you have magic Alfred; I know this because I have magic too," she began.

"How do you know my name?" He was confused and annoyed that he was in the dark about her, but he kept listening.

Beth began to explain that she was the High Sorceress and Protector of the Magical Realms, which was something that he had never heard of before. She went on to explain to him that she was able to do all forms of magic and was in Dragoron to help him to find answers, but she also had a task for him.

"If you can do all forms of magic, what do you need with me?"

"I cannot be everywhere Alfred, I would like you to become my caretaker here for when I am not around, you will be my eyes and ears, and you will be able to call me when you need me," Beth replied.

"Where will you be?"

Beth explained that she would be in her own realm unless needed, she told Alfred that there were many magical realms that needed her protection. She also explained that some of her conversation with him would become foggy and he wouldn't remember the actual words but would remember the sentiment, he would not remember that there were other realms unless she was with him.

'For the wellbeing of the realms, none can discover that the others exist. Each realm has followed its own development path and knowledge of the other realms' existence could influence future decisions," she told him.

Alfred was in shock; he didn't have any idea that there were other places that existed outside Dragoron.

Beth continued to tell Alfred more of the history of the realms, and how she became the High Sorceress. She told him about the source of all magic and the guardian of it. Alfred listened closely and tried to take in every word about the Magic Staff and Mother Nature.

"How will I contact you? I can only do potions; I have no other form of magic," he asked.

"That will not be a problem Alfred, I can give you the ability to contact me through any surface that provides a reflection, it can be a mirror, a puddle, a river, do you get the idea?" she replied.

"You said you could help me get the answers that I need, how will you do that?" he asked her.

"I will come back to the castle with you, I can use my magic to find answers about your daughter Alfred. We will find where she is buried."

"Then I agree, I will be your caretaker."

Chapter 8

"Beth, we will need to get you some different clothes, you don't look like you belong here. We can travel to my sister's home on the way back to the castle, we can trust her."

"No need Alfred, just wait one moment," she replied.

With a flick of her hand, Beth soon dressed in appropriate attire for the realm. Alfred had seen some different forms of magic, but this was very new to him, he was amazed.

"I only have one horse I am afraid; you can ride, I will walk alongside."

"That will not be necessary Alfred, just give me some room, I can sort it out," Beth told him.

Alfred moved away and stood by his horse; Beth positioned herself at the centre of the clearing in the wood near the stream. Alfred watched as she closed her eyes and raised her hands. She pointed her fingers towards the ground, suddenly the earth below his feet began to move.

He thought it felt very odd, he could feel the rumble but there was no sound. The earth began to rise in front of him, a huge amount of earth had formed a mound. Alfred was engrossed watching the shifting earth as it began to take shape. In a matter of seconds a beautiful black stallion had formed and was stood in front of Beth with its head bowed. Alfred was stunned.

"You made a creature from the earth? How did you do that?" he asked.

"As I told you, I am the High Sorceress and I can do all forms of magic, this is just one of the many things I can do, now shall we get going?"

Alfred nodded, he helped Beth climb onto the horse, then get on his own horse and they began to ride back to the castle together.

"I have so many questions to ask you, I have never seen anyone with that much power, are there others like you?"

"I am the only one with my abilities, Mother Nature is also extremely powerful, the magic in my family passes to our daughters, and one day it will be passed on from me, but not to my own children as I have young sons. Hopefully one of them will go on to have a daughter," she replied.

The journey was full of chat, Alfred asked Beth so many questions, he was glad that she had turned up, he felt less alone in his task for answers. He also felt nervous, she would have to hide her magic otherwise the King would find out and he didn't want that to happen.

"You will need to hide your magic when we get to the castle, it won't be safe for you to do any magic, the King has spies everywhere from what I can tell. I will tell people that you are my cousin and that you are visiting from your village," he told Beth.

"I will hide my magic Alfred, don't worry but just know that if I need to use it for any reason, I will be very discreet," she replied. Alfred couldn't help but feel concerned.

In the near distance they could see the castle, Beth rode behind Alfred letting him lead the way to it. Beth had been here before when she was younger as Mother Nature thought she should visit all the realms once she was trained. The castle had not changed, but the feelings inside had. Beth could sense the people's fear and insecurity within its walls.

"What will we do with your horse, will anyone know that it is not real?" Alfred asked.

Beth assured Alfred that nobody would be able to tell that it was not a real animal, so they took both horses to the compound where the animals were kept and left them with the man in charge, who was rather taken with the beautiful black stallion.

Both Alfred and Beth walked into the castle and towards Alfred's rooms, they would need to form some sort of plan to find out what exactly happened to Dalfre, they couldn't rush in asking lots of questions.

"Ok, so where do you want to start?" Beth asked.

"I think we should ask those who were closest to Dalfre, those who took care of her when she was pregnant, they should know where she was taken and buried. At least I hope they do."

"Alfred, while you are asking questions, I think it would be a good idea if I was not visible to anyone, it might stop them talking to you," she replied.

Alfred was still shocked by the manifestation of the horse, now he was being told by Beth that she could make herself invisible, was there anything she couldn't do, he thought.

"I think we should start with her maid, as I have spoken to her before. She couldn't help much but it is worth another try to see if she remembers anything that could help us, even if it is just something small."

"That sounds like the place to start, shall we go now?"

Alfred nodded and Beth raised her hands. Alfred wondered what she was doing. She began to recite some words he had not heard before and then suddenly she was not there anymore.

"Beth, where are you?" Alfred asked, there was a gentle touch on his shoulder which made him jump.

"Alfred, I will keep my hand on your shoulder so you know where I am at all times, shall we go?"

Alfred opened the door; he left it open a little longer than usual to give Beth time to walk through it too. The maid usually worked in the Kings quarters at this time of day, so that is where he decided to try first. There were guards in the castle on the route to the Kings room, they didn't pay him any attention apart from the odd "Hello" as they were used to seeing him in the castle these days. It had not taken long for him to become a fixture in the household, which was to his advantage now.

The door to the Kings chamber was open and Alfred could see the maid busy making his bed, he popped his head through the door and said "hello."

"Hello Alfred, how are you? I haven't seen you for a few days, where have you been?"

Alfred told her that he had a family matter that needed attention, but he didn't go into any detail.

"May I ask you a couple of questions about Dalfre?" he asked her.

"I am not sure what else I can tell you Alfred, I told you all I knew last time we spoke," she replied.

"I know you don't know much, but do you know where her home village was? You said she was taken back there; do you know who took her?"

The maid thought for a moment or two, she told him she wasn't sure where she was from, but she did know that the Knights accompanied the King to the burial.

"Talk to Trystrem, he is one of the Knights, he is the one most likely to answer your questions."

Alfred thanked her then left her to her duties. He could feel Beth still resting her hand on his shoulder, it felt odd knowing that she was there, but not able to see her, he guided her towards the Knights section of the castle.

Alfred wasn't sure that he had met Trystrem before which meant he would need ask someone who he was.

There was a young lad walking down the corridor in the castle, he asked him where Trystrem would be. He told Alfred that the Knights were outside sword training, and that Trystrem was the one in charge. He was one of the best swordsmen in the Knight's ranks. Alfred thanked the lad and went towards the door outside.

Outside in the sunshine he could see a few of the Knights sparring with their swords, one of them was stood watching. Alfred knew from the lad's description that he was Trystrem, it didn't take long to confirm this as him as he was soon guiding the others and giving them tips on how to improve.

Alfred watched the training, waiting patiently for it to be over, despite how eager he was to ask his questions and hopefully fine out where Dalfre was.

Chapter 9

The training seemed to go on forever, but it was only about an hour after Alfred arrived that it finished. Trystrem had noticed Alfred watching them, so he headed over to where Alfred stood as soon as the session was over.

"Did you enjoy the training, are you thinking of joining the Knights?" he asked cheekily, he could see that Alfred was a bit old to be sword fighting.

"I was interested to watch; I have not had the time since I arrived here in the castle. You are all very impressive, the King must feel very safe with you all protecting us," he replied.

Trystrem seemed to recoil slightly when the King was mentioned, both Beth and Alfred sensed the change in him.

"You are the physician, aren't you? You were the one who saved Prince James?."

Alfred told him that he was. Trystrem asked a few more polite questions, mainly about how he was enjoying working and living in the castle. Alfred said that it was something he was getting used to, but that he missed his family and the home he had left behind.

"How long have you been a Knight in the Kings Guards?"

"Quite a few years I lived here as a boy. My father was a Knight before me, becoming a Knight was just something that was expected. There was no other plan as far as my father was concerned, it is a good life," he replied.

"Can I ask you a question?" Alfred said.

"You can, what can I help you with?"

"You were with the King when he took Dalfre back to her village after she died weren't you?"

Trystrem looked quite shocked to be asked, nobody had spoken of Dalfre since she died. He wasn't sure what to say to Alfred, he took a deep breath and thought for a few moments.

"I was not with the King that day, I was told to stay and protect the castle with a few of the novice Knights, those still in training," he replied.

"Do you know the name of the village that they took her too?"

Trystrem was curious why Alfred was asking about her, he was very protective of Dalfre, she was his friend and had been very hurt that the King kept him away from her burial.

"I am sorry Alfred, I cannot help you, I was not told," he answered.

Alfred felt Beth tap on his shoulder, she pulled him slightly, not enough that anyone would notice, but enough that Alfred understood what she meant.

"Thank you for your help, Trystrem, it has been a pleasure to meet you today," Alfred said and excused himself from Trystrem's company.

Both Alfred and Beth walked back to Alfred's rooms, once there Beth became visible again.

"Alfred, I sensed something from Trystrem, I think he was in love with Dalfre. He might just be the one person that could help you find where she is."

Alfred was quite surprised by the suggestion, he did not sense that from Trystrem, but he was sometimes oblivious to things that were in front of him.

"How do I find out?" he asked.

"Trystrem flinched when the King was mentioned, he is not a fan, I think. Maybe you should tell him who Dalfre was, he might just be able to find out where she is from one of the other Knights," she replied.

"What if he tells the King that I am asking questions, he is a vindictive King, look what he is doing to this realm."

"I don't think he will, I don't think he is happy here, it is just where he was told to be throughout his life," Beth said.

Alfred asked Beth if she was hungry, she said that she was, so Alfred went out to the kitchen to get some food from the cook for them both. Once he was back from the kitchen they sat and ate, chatted for a while and it wasn't long before Alfred was showing Beth to a small room with a bed in it for her to sleep. Alfred had an area near the fire in his room that he liked to sleep. They said goodnight.

Beth took a cup of water with her into her room, she wanted to say goodnight to her sons. Once the door was closed, she looked deeply into the cup, and she could see them both in their room. Michael was playing with their dog; he was throwing a ball for him to fetch. Matthew meanwhile was sat scowling at them both, she was worried about her young son, he never seemed to be happy. He seemed to have an issue with the dog, it was as if he was jealous of the time Michael spent playing with it. She knew that she needed to talk to him about it, she needed to find out what was bothering him.

"Good evening boys," she said, they both jumped up from the floor and looked at their mother in the mirror on the wall in their room.

Michael and Matthew told her about their day, Michael was smiling and happy when he was telling her what he had been doing, Matthew just told her what he had done, there was no emotion attached to it.

"When will you be home?" Matthew asked.

"In a few days, I have something to sort out here, but it shouldn't take too long. I miss you both very much," she replied.

Beth chatted for a little longer with them both before saying goodnight to her sons. Wherever she was, Beth always managed to say goodnight to them both before they went to bed. Once they had said goodbye, Beth settled in the small bed and got some sleep. Meanwhile in the other room Alfred was thinking about what Beth had said about Trystrem, he was wondering if he should speak to him again and tell him what he had found out recently about Dalfre.

Alfred tossed and turned in front of the fire, he thought of Dalfre even though he had not met her, he imagined that she looked like her mother Kyra. What bothered him most was how she had died, what had happened to her that night?

Was she really sick or did the King arrange for her death? The thought of it upset him greatly. Eventually slept, but it was not long before the sun was due to rise.

Beth woke Alfred from his shallow sleep when she opened the door from her room. He was exhausted, but at least he had decided what to do about Trystrem.

Chapter 10

"I hope you slept well Beth; it is not the most comfortable bed."

Beth told Alfred that she was comfortable, but she also told him that she had heard him moving around during the night.

"I did not sleep well, I had a lot on my mind, but I have decided to do as you suggested yesterday, I am going to talk to Trystrem today," Alfred told her.

"Would you like me to come with you? I can stay hidden like I did yesterday."

"I would, thank you," he replied.

They sat and enjoyed a hearty breakfast together; Alfred's appetite had not diminished even if his sleep had. Once the food was finished and plates cleared away, both Alfred and Beth left his rooms and headed to the Knights area of the castle again. Today there was no training going on outside, so Alfred needed to find out which room belonged to Trystrem. There were a few people in the corridors so Alfred asked a young Knight apprentice where he could find Trystrem, he was given directions to the room and soon Alfred was knocking on his door.

The door opened quite quickly and a surprised Trystrem said good morning to Alfred, he wondered why he was there.

"May I come in Trystrem? There is something I need your help with," Alfred asked.

Trystrem opened the door wider and gestured for Alfred to enter, which he did with Beth behind him.

"I am a little surprised that you need my help for anything Alfred, I know nothing of healing," he told him.

"Trystrem, I will explain, but before I do, I need to ask if you would keep my confidence. I can't have anyone else knowing what I am going to say to you."

The Knight looked at Alfred closely. He could see that he was nervous and wondered what could possibly make him feel like that, he thought for a moment or two and then agreed to keep whatever Alfred had to say to him secret, if it was not something that would endanger the King. Alfred assured him that it would not.

"Please sit-down Alfred, can I get you anything? Water?" Trystrem asked.

Alfred told him that he would like a water which Trystrem got for him, then he began to tell him the story of his love for Kyra and finding out that he had a daughter.

Trystrem listened and wondered what it had to do with him, he did not understand why Alfred was giving him his family history.

"What has this got to do with me Alfred? I don't understand what I can do for you."

"The daughter I just found out about Trystrem was Dalfre," he replied.

Trystrem was shocked, he felt sorry for Alfred.

"What can I do Alfred?" he asked.

"I need to find out where she is buried, what village she was taken to, I want to visit her grave and say goodbye to my daughter. Can you help me find out where she is?"

Trystrem thought for a moment or two and then told Alfred that he would ask one of the Knights that had accompanied the King. He told him that he would speak to him that day and let him know once he found out.

"Alfred, there is something that you need to know, Dalfre did not love the King, he did not treat her well. I tried to help her; she was planning to leave the castle once the baby was born. I had found them both somewhere to live away from here, a place that they would be safe but a few days before we were due to leave, she died. Alfred, I failed her."

"What can you tell me about my daughter Trystrem? I would love to hear what she was like," he replied.

"Dalfre was beautiful, she had a gentle heart but with an inner strength that I have never seen in anyone before. We were friends and I loved her deeply, in another life..." he began but stopped himself from going further.

"In another life?" Alfred asked gently.

"I loved her Alfred, I just wish that I could have protected her, saved her and I regret that I did not leave the castle with her before the baby was born. I can't look at James, I can't spend time with him, he has her eyes, he has her smile and every time I see him it breaks my heart," he replied.

"Trystrem, would she want you to feel like this, or would she want you to protect and love her son?" Alfred asked.

Trystrem bowed his head, he knew exactly what Dalfre would want.

"I will find you later once I know where she was taken. I only hope that I can find out, it has been kept secret and I don't know why," he replied.

Alfred left Trystrem in his room and went to the nursery to see James, he wanted a cuddle from the young prince, more than ever before he knew that the child was special.

ALFRED'S STORY

Alfred could feel Beth behind him, she squeezed his arm a couple of times reassuringly while he had been talking to Trystrem, now she was with him while he cuddled and played with his grandson. James laughed, smiled and hugged Alfred; he knew that the child loved him.

After spending a bit of time with James, Alfred went back to his rooms and once there Beth made herself visible to him again.

"Trystrem loved Dalfre very much Alfred, I could feel it, he will help you and he will keep it secret for you," she said to him.

Alfred nodded and knew that she was right, he trusted Trystrem even though he had only just met him.

The rest of the day dragged, they stayed in Alfred's rooms out of the way, neither of them wanted too many people to know that Beth was there. Luckily there were no injuries or sickness needing attention that day so they could stay out of sight.

Eventually there was a knock on the door. Alfred opened it to find Trystrem stood there, his face was pale, and he looked shaken.

Alfred told him to come in, which he did, and he sat down.

"Dalfre isn't dead," he announced.

Chapter 11

Alfred was shocked by the revelation from Trystrem, he waited eagerly for him to explain. Trystrem stood quietly in the centre of Alfred's room, staring into space. It looked to Alfred that he was trying to take in the information he had just found out, he gave him a few minutes before asking for more details.

Trystrem had not noticed Beth stood in the room, though she was in the shadows. She moved slightly and made a noise which startled him, he jumped out of his thoughts and stared directly at her.

"It's okay Trystrem, this is my cousin Beth," Alfred said reassuringly.

Trystrem nodded and told Beth that he was honoured to meet her, she told him that she was pleased to meet him too.

"You can talk freely in front of Beth, what have you found out?" Alfred asked.

Trystrem told them both that he had spoken to one of the other Knights, they were good friends, so it was easier than he thought it would be to get the information.

"I told him that I wanted to pay my respects to Dalfre, I said that I had a few days off and while I was on my way to my home village that I wanted to visit her grave," he began.

"He was a bit evasive to start with, but I pressed him on the matter, and he swore me to secrecy before he would tell me. I agreed and we left the castle to find an area that nobody would hear, I didn't understand why it needed to be a secret but went with him."

ALFRED'S STORY

Alfred and Beth listened without saying a word to interrupt Trystrem, he continued with his story.

"When he was sure nobody was around, he told me that the King had asked for some trusted Knights to accompany him on a night ride and that they were told that they could not divulge any details about it, all four of them agreed."

"They were called to the castle once everyone was asleep. The King led them to Dalfre's room where she was asleep with the young prince by her side. The King lifted James away from her and the Knights were instructed to seize her and take her from the castle to a cart that was ready outside, my friend was shocked by this but did as the King ordered him. Dalfre was bound and was told to be quiet for her own safety, apparently she did not do that, he said that she was kicking and screaming as they left the castle, he said he didn't know why they were not heard."

"They got her to the cart; she was taken from the castle to a cabin a few miles away and handed over to a group that were travelling the realm searching for the dragons. They told the King that she would never return, that was the last my friend saw of Dalfre, but he heard that they were travelling north."

"Thank you Trystrem, it looks like I have a mission on my hands now, I just need to find a way to get away from the castle and my duties to the King," Alfred replied.

"I can help with that Alfred," Beth answered.

Alfred was puzzled but he knew that he could not be surprised any more by her capabilities. He asked her what she had in mind.

"Trystrem, I believe that I can trust you, it appears that you love Dalfre and want to find her, but what you must keep secret is that I know of magic, can you keep that to yourself?" she asked.

"My mother had magic Beth, I did not know much about her but that she was a very special woman, your secret is safe with me," he replied.

"Are you both ready?"

Both Alfred and Trystrem told Beth that they were, each of them wondering what she was going to do. They stood and waited for her to tell them but telling them was not what Beth had planned.

There was a blue flash of light, followed by some purple smoke, once it cleared there was another stood in front of Alfred and Trystrem, and no sign of Beth, Alfred and Trystrem were looking directly at another Alfred. The two men were dumbfounded.

"What???" Trystrem started to say but he couldn't seem to complete the sentence.

"I have the ability to appear as another; everyone here will believe that I am Alfred, meaning that he can go in search of Dalfre and take you with him, Trystrem. I can swap between you both while you are away, and nobody will know," she explained.

Trystrem still seemed unable to find the ability to speak and just nodded at what he was being told by Beth, Alfred was just as amazed, but he was still able to speak.

"Can you keep this up for a long time? You might need to," he asked.

"Yes Alfred, I have not actually turned into you, I just give the illusion of being you, so it's not too difficult to keep going. Don't worry about me, you just get your things together and go and find your daughter" she replied. "I can stay here for as long as you need, my family will understand, and I can keep in touch with them."

Both men were very much in shock but agreed with Beth and were soon packing a few things to take with them. Alfred had secretly hidden potions around his body and in a pack, Trystrem went to the armoury and retrieved his sword and a few smaller weapons just in case they needed them. It was not long before they were riding out of the castle on two horses obtained by Trystrem and with Beth's help, all were invisible to anyone they could come across.

"So, North it is then Trystrem!"

"North it is," he replied.

Both men were nervous about what they would discover, but both were determined to find Dalfre.

Chapter 12

Alfred and Trystrem were not sure how far north the group would be, but they knew that it would probably be a few days ride for them to even find their trail. The realm was large, and it was not going to be easy.

"Good luck to you both," Alfred heard in his head, and looking at the expression on Trystrem's face, he heard it too, both knew it was Beth, and neither were surprised.

It wasn't long before they were away from the castle, through the meadows and into the woodlands. The men decided that the mountain ranges would be an ideal place to stop; it would take a while to get there, and so they decided that they would camp the night in one of the many caves. The woodlands were eerily quiet as they rode through, the sun didn't seem able to penetrate the canopy that day, so it was gloomy and quite dark.

For hours they rode through the dense woods. Not one bird sang, no animals stirred; Alfred became very uneasy about it, he had never felt the heavy atmosphere he was feeling that day. It felt like the woods were dying, and all that lived in them were too.

"Alfred, why is it so quiet? Where are the birds and animals?" Trystrem asked.

"I don't know. I have never known anywhere to be this quiet, this dark or this oppressive," he replied.

They carried on riding for another hour or so, through the lifeless woods. Suddenly out of nowhere a bright light shone in front of them with a woman stood at the centre of it. The light felt warm and welcoming but both men were wary of riding towards her. They tried to stop their horses, but they continued closer to her.

"Hello Alfred and Trystrem."

Both men were surprised when she called them by name, and both became more anxious than they already were.

"You don't need to be afraid of me, I am here to help."

"Who are you?" Alfred asked.

"My name is Elnor, and I am the keeper of the forest," she replied.

"Why is the forest so quiet, where is all of the wildlife?" Alfred asked.

Elnor told them that they had all been hidden from view as there was a darkness coming, she said that it was travelling with them both.

"To find the one you are seeking you must save the woodlands and all who reside in them, until you do that you will not be able to pass through them and on to the mountains," she told them.

"How are we supposed to do that, you are the one with magic?" Trystrem asked.

"The darkness needs to be shown the light within you, to dispel it you must open your heart to what you have hidden, Alfred you must show your truth," she answered.

Trystrem looked at Alfred with a puzzled look, he did not understand what Elnor was talking about, though he had not known Alfred long he didn't think that he was hiding anything from him.

"I don't know what you are talking about," Alfred said.

"Alfred until you are honest about who you are, you will not be able to finish your journey through the woods."

Alfred knew what she was referring to, but he was not ready to share with anyone that he was a magical being as well, he had not known Trystrem long enough or well enough to divulge a secret that could get him thrown into a dungeon or executed by the King.

"To dispel the darkness, you must trust the man by your side, I promise that once you do it will dissipate and leave you and the woods in the light," she continued.

Sighing and taking in a deep breath, Alfred wondered what to do, he looked at Trystrem to see what his expression was like, he just looked bemused.

"Alfred, I know we haven't known each other for long, but I can be trusted and to prove it, I will tell you something that I have kept secret from everyone in the castle."

Now it was Alfred's turn to be curious, he wondered what on earth Trystrem could have been hiding.

Trystrem got off his horse, put down his bag and weapons, and stood in front of Alfred. Next, he knelt, his hand on the earth, he muttered something and suddenly, with no explanation in front of Alfred was a beautiful dragon. Alfred knew straight away that it was the magical dragon that everyone thought dead.

"You are Tora, aren't you?" he asked.

"I am. I have been hiding in plain sight for a few years, tracking the Kings plans and helping the magical folk wherever I can. I had to make everyone believe that I was dead; the King needed to think I was gone. I hoped it would protect my kind, but it didn't."

ALFRED'S STORY

"Now you must tell your secret Alfred, you need to be on the side of the light and let this darkness that is infecting your soul go. It began to infect you when you found out about Dalfre. Say it out loud, Alfred," he said reassuringly.

Alfred took a deep breath and began.

"I have magic and I have hidden it for a long time as well. I am angry that Kyra was killed and even more angry that she kept it secret about Dalfre. How could she do that to me? She is my daughter. I had the right to know all about her and be a father to her. I have never known an anger like it, I am raging inside."

"Alfred, I knew of your magic, I could feel it. I know Dalfre has magic too. There is something you should know," Trystrem said.

He began to tell Alfred that the enchantment on Prince James was done by Dalfre, he told him that she knew that her father had magic but not who he was, she knew that he would know how to deal with the enchantment though.

"Dalfre was aware that the King wanted her away from James, she put the enchantment on him to protect him. Once he reached a certain age that spell took hold, he was never in danger, it was just to get you close to him. She wanted you to protect him throughout his young life, she knew she would not be there," he continued.

Alfred didn't know what to say. He had wondered why Dalfre had enchanted her own son, he now knew that she had her reasons, she was protecting her son, making sure someone was with him, somebody that could protect him.

The darkness surrounding Alfred lifted, the sun began to filter through the canopy, the birds began to sing, the woods were alive once more. Alfred could not believe that he was responsible for the darkness, but he did feel much better now he had verbalised his insecurities and anger towards Kyra.

Elnor was looking at them both, she had a wide smile on her face and a look of compassion in her eyes.

"Thank you both, you may now continue through the forest and onto the mountains where you will find what you are looking for."

Tora reverted to the human form of Trystrem, both Alfred and he thought it would be safer to keep the illusion of Tora being dead secret until they needed the force of the magical dragon.

Chapter 13

The two men said farewell to Elnor and continued walking towards the edge of the woods. They could see the snow topped mountains in the distance, they looked beautiful with the blue sky behind them and the sun shining down, the colours were stunning.

A couple of hours later Alfred and Trystrem were at the edge of the trees, they decided to stop for a rest and some food before continuing their journey.

"Alfred, I know you have magic, what are you able to do?" Trystrem asked.

"I am a potion maker," he replied.

"Do you have any with you?"

Alfred told Trystrem that he had various potions hidden on himself and tucked away in his pack, he took out a bottle from his coat, there was no label on it and Trystrem wondered how he knew what it was for.

"What does that one do?" he asked.

"This potion will make an enemy freeze like a statue, I have a truth potion, but that one does not last long, a matter of a couple of days, but I thought I would bring it just in case. I have many more," he replied.

"How do you know what each is for, you have no label?"

Alfred explained that he could tell each potion by the colour, he said that some looked very similar, but each had a slight colour difference. Trystrem nodded as he was told, he was in awe of how Alfred could tell.

Once they had finished their food and rested for a while, both men picked up their packs and continued their journey. The foot of the mountains stretched out in front of them, they began to climb one slowly using a footpath that had been trodden many times by others. The footpath was smooth but occasionally blocked by a fallen rock or two, they moved them out of the way each time and carried on.

The pace was a lot slower in the mountains, but they had travelled further than they thought they would before the light faded. Alfred found a small cave for them to camp the night. It was dry and the opening was protected by some bushes - if the weather was bad overnight, they would at least remain warm and dry. Alfred collected a few sticks and larger bits of wood that littered the ground near the cave and took them back for a fire. Trystrem had collected some ferns and branches for them to sleep on and by the time Alfred had stacked the fire, there were two comfortable beds ready for the night.

"I will light the fire Alfred; it will be a little quicker than you are rubbing two sticks together," Trystrem teased.

Alfred wasn't sure how he would be any quicker than him, but he soon found out, Trystrem knelt by the pile of sticks and logs that Alfred had collected, opened his mouth and suddenly there was a flame directed towards them, instantly there was a fire burning brightly.

"You can still do that in human form?" Alfred hadn't seen that coming.

"I can use all of my abilities in human form, well almost all of them, just don't ask me to fly you anywhere while I am like this," he smiled.

Alfred chuckled. He was happy that he had trusted Trystrem and knew that he had a good friend even though they had only known each other a short time.

Alfred had collected some mushrooms and other wild vegetables on their journey, so once the fire was roaring away, he prepared a vegetable stew for them both for supper.

"That was delicious Alfred, thank you very much."

Alfred told Trystrem that it was his pleasure, he was glad that he had only collected vegetables as he wasn't sure what a dragon in human form liked to eat, so he thought he would be safe with a vegetable stew.

"I eat the same type of things in both forms, I do not eat meat of any form. Contrary to what people say about my kind, we never eat meat, so your vegetable stew was perfect."

Alfred felt relieved and happy that he had chosen a suitable dish to prepare. He thought to himself that he had a lot to learn about dragons.

After dinner was finished both men went to bed on the beds that Trystrem had made; sleep came easily, it had been a long and tiring day.

Trystrem was woken during the night by a noise outside cave. Wondering what it was, he quietly got up from his bed, trying carefully not to wake Alfred. He walked silently from the cave to see what was outside.

As his eyes adjusted to the darkness outside, he soon focused on his friends standing in front of him.

"Agra and Elgar my friends what are you doing here?" he asked them, very happy to see them both.

"My lord, we need to take you to our home, we have captured some people who found us, we are not sure what to do with them," Agra told him.

"I am on a mission to find someone; I am with Alfred the King's physician," he replied.

"We know Alfred, he is a trusted friend of ours. Does he know who you are?" Elgar asked, quite concerned.

Trystrem told them both that he had told Alfred and he explained to them why he was helping him, and that he trusted him completely too. As they were talking Alfred walked out of the cave, he had been woken by the noise they were making, he had recognised Agra's voice.

"Hello again Alfred, Tora has told us what is happening, we may be able to help you," Agra told him.

"We could do with help, but it is not safe for you to be out in the open like this, you know the King has men out searching for you all," he replied.

"That is how we can help, Alfred we captured a group of men that found our home."

Alfred took a few moments, the only group he knew about were the men that Trystrem had told him about, the ones that could have Dalfre, he was nervous to ask.

"Did they have a prisoner with them?" he asked.

"Yes Alfred, a young woman," Elgar told him.

Alfred's heart skipped a beat, his stomach turned over. Could it be his daughter, he wondered?

Chapter 14

"We need to go now and find out if the female prisoner is the person we are searching for" Trystrem said to the other dragons.

Alfred was nervous, excited and worried all at the same time, he was desperate to find his daughter.

"Of course Tora, will you change to your normal form?" Elgar asked.

"No, I will stay like this, if the woman is who we think she is then she knows me, and Alfred needs to be introduced to her. Plus I still need everyone to think that I am no longer alive. Nobody but Alfred must know who I am and that includes the prisoner; she needs to be protected for now," he said.

Both men gathered their things together. Alfred was not sure they would get very far in the dark, but he was soon told by Trystrem that they would be flying. Alfred had not ridden a dragon in the dark, he was a little nervous but trusted his friends completely. Agra and Elgar lowered their heads and knelt in front of Alfred and Trystrem so that they could climb on, it wasn't long before all four were flying over the mountains towards the dragon's home. It was so dark that Alfred wondered how the dragons could see where they were, but in a short time he found out that they could and soon they landed, it really was not that far from where they were camping for the night.

Alfred tried to see where he was, but the moon was not out and there was a lot of cloud cover. It was impossible to make anything out. Once they were down from the Agra and Elgar,

Trystrem grabbed Alfred by the arm and followed the dragons into a damp, dark cave. Eventually after a long walk they could see an opening in front of them, light streamed into the cave from that side. Alfred wondered how one part of the mountain could be in complete darkness and the other side in light.

All four stepped out of the cave and were stood in bright moonlight, and from what Alfred could see they were in a beautiful valley, he couldn't wait to see it in the daylight.

"Where are the prisoners Agra?" Trystrem asked.

"Follow me, the prisoners are being kept over there, we have them locked up and guarded," he replied.

"What about the young woman?" Alfred interrupted.

Agra explained that the woman did not want to be separated from her captors, so she was being held with them. Both Trystrem and Alfred were surprised to hear that.

The four of them were soon stood by the prisoners and the young woman, who had not noticed them coming towards her as she was curled up asleep on a make-shift bed. The others with her did see them coming and were all on their feet, each of them wondering what the dragons were going to do to them.

"I am Trystrem, please tell me who you are?" he said to the man in front of the group.

At that point the young woman woke up and was startled by the site of Trystrem stood in front of her and the group she was with. She jumped up from the bed and pushed her way to the front of the group.

"Trystrem, what are you doing here? How did you find me?" she asked.

Trystrem explained that he had recently found out that she was not dead and that he had decided to look for her.

"How is my son? Is he safe?" she was worried.

"James is safe, the enchantment was lifted by Alfred here, he is a remarkable man Dalfre, but I think you probably know that don't you?" he replied.

Dalfre looked at the man stood beside Trystrem, she could see his eyes, they were her eyes, she could feel his presence and knew immediately that this was the man she had been searching for when she was taken by the King. Once Dalfre knew about her father, she had wanted so badly to find him, and here he was stood in front of her. She was soon overcome with emotion as tears began falling freely down her cheeks.

"Let her out please?" Alfred asked.

Dalfre was soon freed, and the rest of the group secured, she was not happy about that though, or didn't appear to be.

"Please let the rest go, I have not been their prisoner for a long time, they have looked after me well," she pleaded.

"They are dragon hunters, we are dragons, there is a bit of an issue with us letting them go," Elgar replied.

"They have not been hunting dragons for a while, the King just thinks that they are, just like he thinks that they have disposed of me, they are just travellers now, I trust them completely," she told them.

"We only have your word for that, we will talk to them and see what their intentions are and then we will decide from there," he replied.

Trystrem asked Agra if there was somewhere that Alfred, Dalfre and himself could talk privately. Agra showed them back to the entrance to the cave, it was light enough and very private, he told them they would be left alone there. All three thanked him and entered the cave once more.

"Dalfre, do you know who I am?" Alfred asked.

"You are my father," she replied with a smile that lit up her face.

Dalfre was so happy to see him, meeting her father was a dream come true. He walked towards her with his arms open wide, she fell into them, and they hugged for what seemed like a lifetime. Eventually letting go of each other the father and daughter could not stop smiling.

"I never knew about you, Kyra never told me, I had no idea she had given you up, Dalfre I would have hunted for you had I known," he told her.

"I know she never told you, when I found the rest of my family, they told me that they had no idea that I existed, they told me about my mother, but they did not know who my father was. Faren did say that he had an idea who it could be, but just as he was searching for you, I was taken by the King."

Dalfre explained that she hoped that Faren would come and rescue her, but she knew deep down that nobody was able to stand up to the King, so she resigned herself to her fate. Eventually she came to like the King a little, he was kind to her, and she felt comfortable with him. She explained because the King was nice to her she let herself be taken in by him, finally she agreed to become his wife.

"When I told him that I was going to have a baby, he was so caring, nothing was too much trouble, but I did not trust him fully, how could I with all that he was doing here? For just a few moments I let myself believe that he loved me, but he didn't."

"As soon as James was born, he didn't want anything more to do with me, that was when I enchanted my baby as I wanted to make sure he would be protected if I was not with him. I hoped that the man who was my father would know how to break the enchantment, and you did, didn't you? She asked looking at Alfred directly.

"I did. I thought the enchantment was set by your mother, I had seen her cast it before and she told me how to counteract it if ever I came across anyone who was suffering from it. So I went in search of Kyra in case she had escaped her execution by the King," he replied.

"Faren told me that you could be my daughter, and now I have met you, I know that you are, how could you not be?" he was looking at her lovingly, he felt a connection the moment he saw her.

Dalfre asked Alfred about her mother, he did his best to describe the woman who had stolen his heart, the woman who had also broken it when she died, and who had angered him when he found out about his daughter. He missed Kyra so much.

"Dalfre, you say we can trust those with you, are you sure?" Trystrem asked.

Dalfre took her eyes from her father and looked at the man she had fallen in love with while she was in the castle, the man who had no idea how she felt.

"You can, they are a group that were threatened by the King, all they want is to go home and see their families across the mountain pass, he promised that if they got rid of me, he would release them from their hunting duties," she replied.

"Then why are they not home yet, you have been gone from the castle for a long while, surely they should be home now?"

Dalfre looked uncomfortable about the questioning, she did not answer and just shrugged her shoulders. Alfred and

Trystrem were not happy with that response, but neither wanted to push it too much, they were both treading carefully.

Eventually she said that they should ask them, she had just been following wherever they went, she did not know why they had not gone directly home.

Both men decided that they should talk directly to them, but it would be best done in the morning. Everyone was emotional and tired; they needed some rest.

They left the cave and went to find a place to sleep, Agra had already arranged somewhere; there were beds arranged around a large fire for the three of them and it wasn't long before they were comfortable and each trying to sleep.

Sleep evaded all three of them. Too much had happened in such a short space of time, and none could switch off the thoughts rushing through their minds.

Chapter 15

Alfred was up before the sun and was soon joined by Dalfre. Both were a little awkward with each other, it was hard for them to know what to say. The day before had been wonderful for both, but now they needed to start building a relationship and neither wasn't sure where to start.

"I don't know what to call you, it seems wrong to call you Father but that is what you are," Dalfre said to him.

"Call me Alfred, one day you might feel comfortable calling me Father or Dad, I am just happy to get to know you," he replied.

Dalfre smiled, relieved that there was no pressure, she did feel a connection with Alfred, but it was too soon to know how close they would become.

"How was my son when you last saw him?" she asked.

"He is an amazing little boy, I spend as much time as possible with him, he laughs at anything, he is a happy soul and I love him very much," he told her.

"You love him, even though you didn't know he was your grandson until recently?" she queried.

"There was something special I felt from him when I lifted the enchantment, a connection I didn't understand, now I know why."

Dalfre smiled, she was happy that James had Alfred in his life, he needed somebody who cared as much as he seemed to. Alfred went on to tell her that he was crawling around and loved to stand on his feet, he told her that he wasn't frightened of anything.

"I am so glad he is happy; I need to get back to the castle though, he needs his mother and not the man that is his father, he needs to be away from him."

"Dalfre, I don't know how we are going to be able to get him from the King, he is surrounded by guards, and everyone is afraid to confront him," Alfred answered.

Trystrem had been listening to them both chatting, he wanted to help but like Alfred he wasn't sure what they could do, there would be bloodshed if they tried, he knew that for sure.

"I have someone I could ask for help," Alfred told her.

"Who?"

Alfred knew that he shouldn't tell anyone about Beth, but Dalfre was his daughter, she had magic too, he began to tell her what he knew about her and what she was capable of. Dalfre was shocked to know that there was a High Sorceress that could do so much magic. Alfred saw the relief and hope in Dalfre as she took in the information he had given her.

"Do you think she can help?" she asked.

"I do, but we will need to be very careful because if the King finds out he could execute us all" Alfred replied. "I need to contact her, she told me that I could call her using any liquid as a mirror, is there a water source here?"

"Yes, there is a small lake I think, I heard it mentioned when I was captured," she replied.

Trystrem let them both know that he was awake and had been listening to them, he said he would find out from Agra about the lake. He looked deeply into Dalfre's eyes and knew that they must try to get her son from the King, but he knew that it was probably an impossible task. He left them both and went to find Agra.

It didn't take long for Trystrem to find Agra and ask him about the lake, he was soon back with Alfred and Dalfre.

"It will only take us a little while to get to the lake; we will leave after we have eaten breakfast," he told them.

Breakfast was quick, Alfred and Dalfre were eager to contact Beth to see if she could help them. The lake was only a short journey, they were soon stood on its banks. Dalfre and Trystrem stood back while Alfred tried to connect with Beth.

"Beth are you there?" he said while looking directly into the still blue water of the lake, there was no response, he wasn't sure that he was doing it right. Alfred tried again.

"Beth are you there?" he repeated a few more times, suddenly he saw her face clearly in the water.

"I am here Alfred, did you find Dalfre?" she asked.

"I have, she is safe and here with me. Beth, we need your help still, can you help us get James away from the King?"

Beth was taken aback by the request; she had come to the realm to see that it was settled, her involvement with Alfred was unplanned and she wasn't sure that Mother Nature would be impressed with her meddling in the realm with her magic. Beth knew that she would be in danger if it was found out that she had magic and had used it against the King, the rightful ruler of the realm, even if he was a mean and vengeful man.

"I can try Alfred, though it could be challenging," she told him.

"You just want to get James back to Dalfre, nothing more?" she asked.

Alfred told her that their only plan was to get James back to his mother, back in her arms where she could love and protect him.

"I need to see if it is okay for me to get involved in this Alfred, I am a protector and I can only usually intervene if the realm is under attack from outside forces. The running of the realm is not my business, it needs to develop and change at its own speed," she told him.

"I understand Beth, I will wait here for you," he replied.

Beth said goodbye to Alfred and immediately contacted Mother Nature for her advice, she needed her experience and knowledge to guide her. Once she was able to talk to her, she told her about what had been happening in the realm, Mother Nature was not impressed that Beth had become as involved as she was, she reminded her that it was not her business to influence the politics or development of any realm.

"Beth, you know that we are here to protect the whole of the Magical Realms, if we got involved in any of the day-to-day issues, we could influence their natural progression," she told her.

"But the King is killing the dragons, he is wiping out magic here, can't I get involved to stop that?" she asked.

"Magic will survive in the realm Beth, there will be a future for it there, for now you must not intervene in how the King rules. I promise there will be peace and magic again in Dragoron," she replied.

Beth knew that removing the King was the only way for peace in the realm, she was disappointed that Mother Nature would not let her try, she did tell Beth that she could help James become the King he was destined to be in other ways but with no detail. Beth was told that she could help reunite Mother and Son, but that she had to be creative and not cause the monarchy to collapse. A little disappointed with the constraints being put on her she said that she would try her best.

Beth began to call out to Alfred, who answered her immediately, hopeful that she would be able to help them.

Chapter 16

Alfred introduced Beth to Dalfre who was excited to think that she could be with her son very soon. The look on Beth's face soon dispelled that hope.

"Mother Nature will not allow me to help you take James from the King. We must come up with a way to reunite you both, but the King must not find out," she told them both.

"Why can't we?" Dalfre asked tearfully.

"We cannot destabilise the monarchy, but we must ensure that James becomes the King he should be. That means getting you into the castle to teach him as he grows, to give him the values that he will not get from his father," Beth replied.

"How will we do that? There is no way to get me back in the castle safely or anywhere near James," she said.

"We will find a way, we have to," Alfred told her.

All agreed that there must be some way to get Dalfre back to her son, but none of them had any idea how. It would take a lot of thought.

Alfred and Dalfre said they would contact Beth if they came up with anything, but in the meantime they decided that they needed to talk to the prisoners that were sent by the King to kill the dragons and dispose of Dalfre.

Trystrem guided them both back, he had listened quietly to what was being said, and knew that he could help Dalfre.

"You are very quiet Trystrem, are you okay?" Dalfre asked.

"I am okay, I just have a lot on my mind, but it will all get sorted in time," he replied.

ALFRED'S STORY

Once back from the lake Trystrem excused himself from the two of them and went off to find somewhere quiet to think, he asked Agra to join him, he needed his counsel.

"Can you take me somewhere that we won't be interrupted, Agra?" he asked.

"Jump on, I know just the place," he replied.

Agra flew out over the lake and a little beyond to a clearing in a small woodland at the edge of the dragon's home. He gently landed on the grass which was doused in beautiful sunlight.

"What a beautiful spot Agra, this is just perfect," he told his friend.

"What is wrong Tora?" he asked using Trystrem's given name.

Trystrem swore Agra to secrecy before he told him, Agra agreed. He began to recite the conversation between Alfred, Dalfre and Beth to Agra who was troubled by what he heard. He knew that Dragons would be persecuted until the day the King was no longer on the throne.

"What can we do?" he asked.

"I have an idea, but first, I need to make sure that there is no other way; that is why I need to talk to you. This will impact on all our kind," he replied.

Trystrem told Agra that he thought the only way to save the dragons was to make sure that Prince James grew up without the King completely influencing him with his views on magic and on his feelings about Dragons.

"We are peaceful, it is not us that started the ill feeling with the King, even as a child he was causing us issues, how do we counteract that?" Agra asked.

"We have to ensure that his son does not fear us, we have to help Dalfre, and Alfred achieve that."

"That will not be an easy thing to do, Dalfre is known in the castle, she will be captured as soon as she sets foot there."

"I can only think of one-way Agra, and it will need your blessing, you will need to protect our kind when I can't," he replied.

Agra was getting worried; he had no idea what Trystrem was thinking.

"The magic I use to keep hidden in the form of man is strong,l" he began.

"I have heard that in our past a dragon could stay in this form by giving his magic to another, I am thinking of giving my magic to Dalfre so that she can change her appearance and be with her son," he continued.

Agra was shocked, he had heard the same thing, he never imagined his friend would ever consider giving his magic away.

"Once you do that, you would never be able to get it back, and you know the consequences to both you and Dalfre don't you?" he asked.

Trystrem nodded, he knew exactly what it would mean.

"Please think about this Agra, you will have to take on much more responsibility, I will still be able to warn you about things, but I won't be able to protect you anymore with magic."

"There is no other way?" he asked.

Trystrem told him that he couldn't think of any other way, but he would still try to find another one if he could. Agra agreed to think about what he was proposing.

Both Trystrem in human form and Agra the dragon sat in the clearing for a long while, each thinking deeply about alternatives, but neither could find one. Eventually as the sun dropped in the sky, they looked at each other, nodded and knew that it was the only way they could help Dalfre and ultimately secure the future of the Dragon kingdom.

"It is time to get back to the others, we know what we must do now," Trystrem said.

The flight back was quick, they were soon landing, Alfred and Dalfre were sat by a fire, both deep in thought, each of them looked sad Trystrem thought, he hoped his plan would change that for them. It would be a sacrifice, but one he was willing to make for the woman he loved deeply.

Agra stayed where he was as Trystrem made his way across to join the pair by the fire. He thought it best to give the group some privacy whilst Trystrem explained how the next steps would impact them.

Chapter 17

Dalfre looked up and saw Trystrem walking towards them. He looked troubled, which made her nervous. As he sat next to her at the fireside, she watched the orange glow from the roaring flames light up his face. She wanted to tell him how she felt about him, but she knew that it would never be possible; she was an outcast with a death sentence from the King and nothing they could do would change that.

"I have a solution," he stated.

"You do? What is it? Will I be able to get my son away from the King?" Dalfre could not contain her excitement, all other thoughts fell away.

"First Dalfre I must show you something, it will be quite a shock for you."

Alfred knew what he was talking about, he took Dalfre's hand in his and squeezed it, she looked at him and saw a reassuring smile.

Nervously, she turned back towards Trystrem who now stood up from the fire and walked away from them. He turned around and looked directly at Dalfre. Almost instantly there was something different about Trystrem Dalfre thought, her eyes still locked with his.

He broke the stare and Dalfre found herself looking at the most majestic creature she had ever seen. The creature had Trystrem's eyes ... but what she saw was impossible! How could the man that was stood in front of her now be a dragon?

"How?" she asked, not sure what else to say.

"Dalfre, I am Tora, the magical dragon. To ensure the safety of my fellow dragons, and so that the King believed me to be dead; I have been hiding amongst you in human form."

Dalfre was not sure what to say, she never imagined that anything like that was possible. Yes there was magic that could do wonderful things, but to be able to change form.

That was something that she would have never thought of, ever. Tora changed back into his human form, and they began to talk about his suggestion.

"Can you do other magic that can help me get James?" she asked him.

Trystrem took a deep breath and began to tell them a story about a Dragon that gave up his magic so that he could stay in human form. He did not go into the fine detail of the story, just that it was possible.

"What are you suggesting? Are you thinking about giving up your magic?" Alfred asked him.

Trystrem told him that he couldn't think of another way to get Dalfre to her son, he said that he would investigate other possibilities. He asked Alfred if he knew of anything else that could help.

"Let me contact Beth, she might know something," he replied.

"If you give up your magic, there will be no magical dragon in the realm to protect the others," Dalfre said.

"I know, I have discussed it with Agra, he knows what the consequences are, and he will protect them," he replied.

"What will happen to you if you give up your magic?" Alfred asked.

"I will choose what form to live the remainder of my life in, then I will build a life around that," he replied.

"You can choose?" Dalfre asked.

"Yes, I can Dalfre, I can choose to live amongst my friends in Dragon form, or I can live as Trystrem," he replied.

Dalfre's heart skipped. She hoped he would choose to live as Trystrem, she did not dare ask him though.

"What would happen if you gave up your magic, how does it help? I am a little confused," she asked.

"Dalfre, if I give up my magic, it is so that you can be changed in appearance and live close to your son. We could get you back into the castle to be near him every day. As we cannot take him from the King, we must find another way for you to guide him. You heard what Beth said," he replied.

"James would never know who I was though, would he?"

"No he would not, but he would know that he was deeply loved by the woman who raises him in the castle, we could make that happen." He took hold of her hands and looked into her eyes. "Alfred has the King's trust and could get you in as his maid, his teacher or another role where you would be with him."

Alfred thought the plan could work, but he said he would speak to Beth to see if there was an alternative first. He left Dalfre and Trystrem by the fire and wondered back towards the lake to contact her. It didn't take long to get there, and he was soon explaining to Beth what Trystrem had said.

"Alfred, let me talk to Mother Nature, stay here I won't be long," she said.

Alfred sat by the lake pondering everything that he had been told, he wanted so much for his daughter to see her son grow into a man. He already knew that she would be a wonderful guide for him; he hadn't known her for long, but Alfred already loved her deeply and could see the strength that she had.

It did not take long for Beth to get back; he could see that she was troubled.

"What is it Beth?" he asked.

"Mother Nature cannot think of anything else that could be done, her magic and mine could not keep Dalfre looking different permanently. The only magic that could do that is Dragon magic, but you need to know the repercussions, you need to talk to Trystrem and get him to explain what they are," she replied.

"I will, thank you Beth."

Alfred went back to his daughter and Trystrem, both sat in silence at the fireside and looking into the flames. They looked up as he approached.

"Beth has no other way; it seems, Trystrem, that your suggestion is the only way to keep Dalfre safe and with James. Beth told me that we need to know the repercussions of this though, what are they?" he told them.

He looked at Dalfre. "When I give up my magic and take whichever form I choose, from that moment my remaining life will be limited. I will know exactly how long I have left to live. But it is not just me, if you accept my magic then the same happens to you."

"Limited? How long will we have?" she asked.

"From the moment it happens, we will have twenty years to live. Not a moment longer. There will be no way to avoid it," he replied.

"Twenty years? How? Why?" Alfred asked.

"I cannot answer that Alfred, it is just the way it is. I can only think that it was decided long ago to act as a deterrent, to make us think long and hard before we gave up our magic," he replied.

Dalfre was shocked. How could she ask Trystrem to give up his life? Dragons live for many years, and she would be taking that from him, she did not even know if she could give up her own life after twenty years with her son. There was so much to think about, she needed time.

She stood up and both men looked up at her expectantly.

"I can't make this decision quickly, nor should you Trystrem. There is too much to think about. I cannot make this decision right now." Tears trickled down her cheek as she turned and left. She had never had anyone offer such a huge sacrifice in her life.

She needed to be alone, both men understood and watched her walk away.

Chapter 18

Alfred and Trystrem chatted for a bit longer about what would happen if Dalfre agreed to accept the magic from Trystrem.

"Twenty years is not long; can you really give up the rest of your life for a woman and child that are not connected to you?" Alfred asked.

Trystrem paused for a few moments, he had not admitted to anyone how he felt about Dalfre, and he was about to spill it all to her father.

"I love her, I have loved her from the moment I first met her in the castle, I was one of her guards when she first arrived," he told Alfred.

"Does she know how you feel?" he asked.

Trystrem shook his head, he had never thought that he could tell her, after all he was a magical dragon and she was a human, how could that have ever worked? But now he knew that if she agreed he would be taking on human form permanently and that gave him hope.

"You need to tell her, if she knew that you felt that way it could help her decide. It could go one of two ways, she might tell you that she loves you too and say no to you giving up the rest of your life, or she could say yes and want to spend the twenty years with you and her son. One thing is certain, you will never know unless you tell her, Trystrem."

"I need to go and find her, don't I?" he replied.

"Not yet, give her time to digest what has been said so far, it is a lot to take in. It's not often you meet a dragon that can live as a man," he said smiling at Trystrem reassuringly.

The two men sat by the fire waiting for Dalfre to come back, it felt like hours to them both, but eventually she walked back into view with a deep thoughtful look on her face, neither of them could gauge what decision she might have made, if any at all.

"Do you have any more questions?" Trystrem asked as Dalfre sat down by the fire, she shook her head and told them that she didn't want to discuss it then, they decided to leave it and just eat something and get some rest.

Trystrem was desperate to talk to Dalfre, he knew that he needed to wait a little longer, what difference would another few hours make when he had waited so long already?

Alfred looked at them both, each had the weight of the heavens on their shoulders. He knew that they both had things that they needed to discuss, he hoped that whatever decision they made that they would be happy with it. Whatever they settled on, it was not going to be an easy road to travel.

After they had eaten Alfred excused himself and left the two of them by the fire, he hoped that they would use the time to talk.

"Goodnight both of you," he said and then hugged Dalfre tight before leaving her alone with Trystrem.

Dalfre and Trystrem sat silently looking into the fire for a while, eventually Dalfre spoke.

"Why would you give up your life for me Trystrem?" she asked.

Trystrem took a deep breath, he knew that he had to tell her now, he could not hide it from her any longer.

"Because Dalfre, I love you," he replied looking directly into her eyes.

Trystrem saw tears forming at the corners of her deep blue eyes, eyes that he had lost himself in many times. Dalfre stared back at him, she held his gaze for a long time and could feel the tears falling down her cheeks.

"Trystrem, I can't ask you to give up everything for me, you would resent me for asking you," she replied to him.

"You have not asked. I offered Dalfre, because I want to help you be with your son, you deserve that. And it was an easy solution to offer because I love you. I would rather have twenty years watching you raise him than live the rest of my life knowing that you were parted," he replied.

Dalfre stood up from where she was sat, she walked over to Trystrem and knelt in front of him, she raised her hand and gently placed her palm on his cheek. She looked at him, smiled and then kissed him gently on the lips and said, "I love you too."

Trystrem thought how beautiful she looked in the warm colours from the flames of the fire, his heart swelled when she told him the words he had longed for. He took her hand and stood up, brought her close to him and put his arms around her waist and kissed her again. They were both so happy.

Both spent the night talking about shared memories from the castle and the moments that they both wanted to admit their feelings but couldn't. They were both happy that each other finally knew what was in their hearts.

The sun began to rise casting a beautiful glow in the distance that coloured everything with a golden hue. It was going to be a beautiful day, but one with a lifechanging decision to be finalised. They had not spoken anymore about it during the night since they had discovered their love for each other.

Alfred woke and went to see how his daughter was. He found her where he left her the night before, with Trystrem by her side. Alfred could see the smiles on their faces, he knew that Trystrem must have told Dalfre how he felt, it made Alfred happy, but would Trystrem still be happy if she said no to the plan?

"Good morning both of you, how are you both today?" he asked with a wry smile on his face, he didn't need an answer.

"Good morning, can I get you some breakfast?" Trystrem asked, the smile still not leaving his face.

"Yes please," he replied.

Trystrem left Dalfre and Alfred together, Dalfre told him about their conversation the previous night, she told her father that she loved Trystrem too.

"How can I let him do this?" she asked him.

"If you had the choice of spending a life without James and Trystrem or twenty years with both of them, which could you live with?" he replied.

"I would choose the twenty years with them both, but it's not fair that I must choose that, nor that Trystrem will give up so much for me. There must be another way, there just must," Dalfre replied, tears forming again.

"There is no other way Dalfre. The King must remain in power, and you must guide James. The only way to do that is if you change the way you look, and Trystrem wants that for you. I will be by your side too; I can help you both through this," he said to her.

Trystrem came back with some food for them both, which they ate in silence. Dalfre took time to think about what Alfred had said to her, she knew deep down it was the only way she could be with her son, so the answer had to be yes.

"Trystrem, the answer is yes. How do we do this? How do you give me your magic?" Dalfre asked.

Trystrem was pleased that Dalfre had decided to accept his offer, he knew that the safety and future of the realm depended on it.

Chapter 19

"Legend says that to give away dragon magic I must travel to the cave of the first magical dragon in a place called Ellmere" he began "You will need to come with me, but it is not certain that I can give you my magic. You will have to prove your worth to the spirit of the original dragon."

"Alfred, will you come too? I will ask Agra as well," Trystrem asked.

"Of course I will, I don't want to be parted from my daughter, not now that I know about her. She will have me by her side, always," he answered.

Dalfre seemed nervous to Alfred, he put his arm around her shoulder. She rested her head on his, it was going to be a trying time. A quest.

"How do I prove myself to the first dragon? What will I have to do?" she asked.

Trystrem told her that he did not know. He explained that he only knew of one other dragon who had given away their magic, he didn't know what the recipient had to do. The legend didn't say.

"How do we get to Ellmere?" Alfred asked.

"We will fly, it is in the far north of the realm, hidden from all but me. Agra does not even know where it is, so I will be breaking a vow by taking him there; but he will need to know so that he can protect the legend, and he will need to bring us back," he told them.

'The journey will take two days of flight; it will be tiring for us both. We will need to keep away from any of the groups the King has sent out to kill the dragons; hopefully there won't be many that far away from the castle, but we just won't know until we begin."

Trystrem told them both that they would set out immediately, he said that there was no time to waste, the sooner the magic is transferred the sooner Dalfre would be by the side of her son. He went to talk to Agra and left them both to gather their things together. There was not much to get, just Alfred's pack and potions, Dalfre did not have anything with her when she was found with the group she was travelling with.

When Trystrem got back he was joined by Agra.

"Are you ready?" he asked.

"Before we go, what is happening with the people I was travelling with? Will they be freed?" Dalfre asked.

Agra told her that he had ordered their release in the following few days, he said that once the four of them were far away from the camp they would be taken by the dragons back to their own homes. They would not know the route of journey as it would be done on a dark and moonless night to protect the location of the dragon's home. Dalfre was happy that they would be back home with their families, and away from the King.

"It is time to go, are you ready?" Agra asked.

"Just one thing left to do," Trystrem replied.

A moment later Trystrem was in his dragon form, Agra bowed before him, he knew that this could possibly be the last time that he saw his friend as Tora the only Magical Dragon.

"Alfred, you climb onto Agra, I will take Dalfre, hold on tight both of you," he said.

As soon as they were sat on the necks of the dragons, they took flight, flying directly up towards the clouds, both Dalfre and Alfred held on so tight, they were afraid of falling off. The speed that the dragons took off was a lot quicker than expected; they travelled almost vertically, which was not the most comfortable take off for their passengers. It wasn't long though, until they levelled off above the clouds.

The four of them flew for a few hours, high above the clouds so that they would not be seen on the ground, nobody wanted to be discovered. The sky above the clouds was a beautiful pale blue, the sunshine bounced off the clouds giving them a magical feel. Tora and Agra began to descend, both Alfred and Dalfre felt the temperature change as they went through the cloud; it was much colder and they could feel the dampness of them, even the white fluffy clouds contained moisture, and both were a little wet by the time they landed.

"We will take a short break and then get back to our journey, I want to be halfway there before it gets dark," Tora told them all.

They spent a little while eating, drinking and the dragons rested but as Tora said, they were soon back travelling towards the cave of the original magical dragon. The afternoon passed as quickly as the morning had, flying high above the clouds meant that Alfred and Dalfre were disorientated, there were no landmarks to see with the cloud cover.

Once the light started to fail Tora and Agra landed again, they were in the middle of a woodland, a clearing by a stream was the home for the night.

"Will we arrive before nightfall tomorrow?" Alfred asked.

ALFRED'S STORY

"If we have a good journey like today and set off earlier, we should be there by late afternoon, Dalfre and I can then enter the cave together," Tora replied.

"Can I come in too?"

"No Alfred, I am afraid you will need to wait outside with Agra. The magic is not to be revealed to anyone other than those involved. I know you want to be with Dalfre, but I can't allow it this time, she will be alright, I promise I will protect her," he answered.

Alfred was disappointed, he could see the nervousness in her eyes, he smiled at her, trying his best to reassure her.

"Get some rest, we will leave as soon as the sun rises in the morning," Tora advised.

The four of them slept soundly in the clearing, it only seemed like a few moments to Alfred before the sun was rising in the sky, he was the last to wake, Dalfre was waiting impatiently to go.

"Are you all ready? Shall we set off?" Agra asked.

Alfred could feel the excitement, apprehension and tension in the group, each one feeling something different. He climbed on Agra, Dalfre was already sat on Tora waiting for the take off, but this time the dragons took of gently, checking the surroundings as they went.

The day passed just as the previous one, flying high above the clouds, stopping for a short rest and back in the sky again. All were relieved that they had not encountered anyone on their journey.

Quite abruptly Tora announced that they had reached their destination and descended at speed, Dalfre holding on tight. Agra followed him at the same speed. They landed at the base of a huge snow topped mountain, the grey granite of it shining in the sunshine. It was a beautiful sight.

"Agra, Alfred, can you please move away from here a little? I am afraid that I cannot allow you to see the entrance, nor how I open it," Tora asked.

Before they did as he asked, Alfred took Dalfre's hand in his and squeezed it tight.

"I love you Dalfre, you are a brave and wonderful woman, Tora, I cannot thank you enough for this, I am very proud to call you my friend," Alfred said to them both.

Agra bowed in front of Tora, and then the two majestic dragon's foreheads met, each knowing that they would never meet again in this way. It was the last moment Agra would ever be near Tora again.

Alfred and Agra left as they had been requested; Tora turned to Dalfre.

"Are you ready Dalfre?" he asked.

"Yes, I am," she replied.

Chapter 20

"Step back a little, I need to open the entrance," he told Dalfre.

Dalfre did as he asked, she watched Tora as he gently blew a flame towards the granite, the flame was not the colour she was expecting, it was a beautiful shade of purple and there was no heat, she was amazed by it, it was a truly magical flame.

Suddenly there was a thundering noise as stones fell from the mountain above, none of them near Dalfre or Tora. Then the granite in front of them began to move, slowly at first, with cracks appearing in front of them. Soon, the area disintegrated into small stones, leaving a pile on the ground, and a huge opening in front of them.

"Follow me," Tora told her.

Dalfre followed Tora into the darkness of the cave and towards the uncertainty of what she was to face.

Alfred and Agra heard the thundering noise, but stayed where they were, neither wanting to jeopardise what was happening, but both hoping that it was nothing to worry about.

As they walked deeper into the cave, Dalfre followed Tora closely, though she could barely see him in front of her. The darkness was like nothing she had ever experienced before, the air was heavy and thick and her breathing felt laboured. She felt like she was wading through water.

Within minutes Dalfre was collapsed on the wet rocky ground in the cave, she was unconscious. Tora heard her fall and retraced his steps to gently pick her up. He continued, carrying her further into the cave.

Dalfre did not move, she was completely unaware of what was happening to her. Tora swallowed down his uncertainty. He knew that it was necessary for Dalfre to go through this. That the legend and the magic needed to be protected. He knew that she was being tested already. He continued towards the centre of the cave, towards the source, towards the spirit of the first magical dragon.

"Dalfre, do you see me?" a voice asked in the darkness.

"I don't see anything, is that you Trystrem?" she replied.

"No, it isn't, my name is Adriana, and I am the dragon you seek," the voice replied.

"Why can't I see you? It is so dark."

"Dalfre, this is the beginning of your journey, the test begins here. I know that Tora wants to give you his magic, but I need to know that you are worthy of this. Our magic is precious; he must trust and love you very much to give up his destiny for you," Adriana said.

Dalfre was shocked, she did not realise that Tora would be giving up his destiny, she could not ask him to do that for her, even if it meant that she would be with her son as he grew up.

"What is his destiny?" she asked.

"That is not your concern, that is between the magical dragons of the past, present and the future, we need to know that you understand that he will be giving up his."

"I cannot ask him to give up his destiny, I love him, and I would not want to be responsible for that. He is a very special person in my life, I couldn't take his future from him," she replied.

Suddenly Dalfre was blinded by light burning through her eyelids, she gently opened them, she was squinting, her eyes were watering badly, unable to make out anything in the cave. Eventually she began to focus, she could see Tora in front of her, he was stood by a large circular rock, it was a form of altar, and in the middle of it was a bright orb the same colour as the fire Tora used to open the cave. He was talking to it, but she could not make out what he was saying.

Dalfre got up. Tora heard her moving and turned towards her and smiled.

"Come here Dalfre, it appears that the spirit of Adriana would like to meet you in person, so to speak," he said.

Dalfre wondered what had happened, she had already spoken to the magical dragon. Or had she? Everything was becoming muddled.

"Don't worry, you have already met in your unconscious state, I believe that you passed the first test, there is just one more thing to do," he said reassuringly.

"Hello again Dalfre, because you were unwilling to accept that Tora wanted to give up his destiny, it shows me that you have a great heart. It tells me that you are not prepared to put your wants above another person's destiny. So for me to agree with Tora's request you must now prove one more thing, are you ready?" Adriana asked.

"I cannot accept this; I will not take away his destiny," she replied.

"Dalfre, this is my destiny, I promise. You are not taking away anything. I am giving it willingly," Tora told her.

Dalfre looked deeply into his eyes, she could see that he was telling her the truth, she trusted him more than ever in that moment. She hoped that he would stay in her life after he gave her his magic.

"Then I am ready for the next test," she replied after a few moments.

"The next test is a choice Dalfre, it may not be an easy one for you to make," Adriana told her.

Dalfre took a deep breath and waited for Adriana to tell her what it would be.

"To accept the magic from Tora you must give up something that you value the most. There are two options for you to choose from, firstly I know that you dream of having many children Dalfre, I know that you wanted a large family because you never had that. For you to have this magic, you will have to give up that dream. There will be no more children in your life, and James will never know you are his mother. Or you will give up the love of your father, the man you never knew until recently, he will never know that you existed, he will only know you as another employee of the King," she said.

The choices given to her were so difficult; she already loved Alfred, she couldn't give that up, but she also wanted lots of children too. How could she choose between the two?

"You must choose now Dalfre, there is no time to think, which will it be?" Adriana pushed.

Dalfre was torn, should she choose the love she already has or the love of children she could have in the future?

"Now Dalfre!" Adriana insisted.

"I will keep the love of my father and give up my chance to have more children," she replied instantly, knowing that she could not lose the man she had just found.

"A wise choice. Lastly, you know that from the moment the magic is given to you, a countdown begins; you and Tora will only have twenty years, the moment that time is reached you will both die, and the next magical dragon will be born," she continued.

"Will you accept this?" she asked them both.

Tora and Dalfre both replied "Yes" to Adriana.

"Your appearance will be different to everyone but your family, Tora and Agra; you will still see your own reflection when you look in a mirror, do you accept this as well?"

Dalfre said that she did, she was glad she would still see her own face.

A moment later, there was a bright purple flash. It was blinding, and it took Tora and Dalfre a few moments to adjust to the light again once it dimmed. When they did manage to see they were no longer in the cave, they were stood at the entrance, which was now sealed again. Tora was in human form and no longer a dragon.

"My magic is gone; I can feel it," he told her.

Dalfre embraced him, the man she loved deeply.

Chapter 21

Alfred and Agra saw the blinding light, they were both unsure whether to go to it or wait and see. They didn't have to wait long.

Trystrem and Dalfre were soon walking towards them. Alfred was confused; Dalfre still looked the same, yet Trystrem was in human form.

Dalfre ran and hugged her father, she had a huge smile on her face, Alfred hoped that meant that it had worked. Trystrem explained to them that they would always see Dalfre as she was, he told them that others would not.

"The next issue is going to be getting Dalfre into the castle and near James," Alfred said.

"I have a solution for that," Trystrem announced.

Everyone waited for him to explain, he didn't, instead he turned to Dalfre.

"Dalfre, you know that I love you. I hope you love me as much as I do you," he began.

Dalfre told him that she did, she told him that she loved him very much.

"Then, would you marry me, would you become my wife?" he asked.

She was a little taken aback, they had only just told each other how they felt, but she also knew that she only had twenty years left to live. She didn't need time to answer though, she loved Trystrem and wanted to spend those twenty years with him, James and her father.

"I would be honoured Trystrem but, is this just so that I can get into the castle, because you have already given up so much for me?" she replied.

Trystrem told her that it wasn't, he explained to her that it was because he loved her and wanted to spend his life with her.

"Then yes, I will marry you," she told him.

Alfred and Agra were shocked but in a good way, they both knew that Dalfre and Trystrem belonged with each other.

"On the way back we will travel to Farren's village and then to mine, you can meet your aunt and her family, you can marry there," Alfred told them.

"Shall we start back on our journey home?" Agra asked.

All of them agreed that they should, Agra knelt and told them all to climb on his back. Once they were settled he took flight, easily managing to carry all three. He was a large and strong dragon.

"What about keeping the cave secret, we will see the way home?" Alfred asked Trystrem.

"The only one who will remember where the cave is located will be Agra, he will be the caretaker of the cave until a new magical dragon is born. He will guide that dragon here, just like I was guided as a young dragon," he replied.

"Agra will take us to a safe place near Farren's village Alfred, there is a clearing that will be safe for him to land, it won't take long," he continued.

Trystrem was right, it did not take long for Agra to get them close to Farren's village and they were soon landing. Each of them climbed down and onto the soft wildflower filled meadow in the middle of the woods, a beautiful place filled with dappled sunshine.

Dalfre and Alfred thanked Agra and left him and Trystrem to say their goodbyes. It was a sad time for the dragons, they no longer had the protection of the only magical dragon, but Trystrem would try his best to warn them of any dangers heading their way.

"Thank you for everything my dear friend, I am sorry to leave all of the responsibility on your shoulders, but you are a great leader and I know that you will protect everyone," Trystrem told him.

"I am honoured that you trust me, I will not let you down. You know how to call me if you need me. For now my Lord Tora, goodbye," he replied with dragon tears running down his face.

Agra nuzzled his friend, turned away and flew high up into the blue sky, leaving him behind. Dalfre saw that Trystrem was upset, she walked towards him and could see they hurt in his eyes, she felt guilty for that, but he hugged her and told her that he loved her.

"Let's get going, Farren will be so happy to see you and I can't wait for you to meet my sister, Dalfre. Helen will love you and so will her husband and boys," Alfred said.

The three of them walked out of the woodland and were soon on the outskirts of the village, all three shocked at the sight in front of them. The village was burnt to the ground, every single building virtually destroyed. Every person gone.

"What happened here? Where is everyone?" Dalfre asked.

Alfred said nothing, but deep down he knew that the King had been on another rampage. Only he and his men had ever left this type of destruction in the realm, nobody else.

ALFRED'S STORY

"We need to get to my village; I must check that my sister is safe. If this has happened here other villages could also have been attacked," Alfred said to them.

All three were devastated by the destruction they had discovered, each hoped that it was the only village that had been attacked, all of them wondering if the villagers had got away safely.

They began the walk to Alfred's home, all downhearted and nervous about what they would find.

Chapter 22
Beth

As soon as Alfred and Trystrem left the castle Beth took on each of their forms, trying her best to keep up the appearance that they were both still in the castle. Luckily there were not many calls on her for medical treatment, but the training that Trystrem did each day was exhausting.

Beth kept an eye on Alfred's progress using her magic, she was glad that he had found Dalfre.

The King seemed more unhappy than usual, and his mood continued to darken as time went on. Rumour around the castle began to spread that he had found out that magic was being practiced in the outlying villages. Of course, he had no proof, but the whispers that had reached his ears were enough to enrage him.

Beth made sure that she stayed close to the Knights. If there was going to be trouble, she knew that they would be the first to be called on by the King.

A few days after Alfred and Trystrem had left, the Knights were summoned by the King. She entered the main hall with them, disguised as Trystrem.

"Trystrem! I need you to take some of the Knights, magic is being used in my realm! I have been told of two villages that are using it. In one of the villages, an elder by the name Farren is openly using it to encourage a rebellion. The other village has agreed to help him. These thoughts of rebellion must be extinguished immediately. I want the inhabitants of both villages arrested and put in the dungeons then tried for treason. Destroy their homes. We shall send a clear message to anyone else that might have forgotten that I WILL NOT TOLERATE MAGIC IN MY KINGDOM!"

The King seemed worryingly unhinged.

Beth knew that Farren was not magical, she knew that the village was innocent and that she must do something to protect them from the King. The King had also mentioned the other village, after a quick discussion with one of the other knights she realised it was the home of Alfred's sister and her family. She knew that they were not plotting against the King, they were just trying to live a quiet life.

The King continued to rant when he eventually stopped Beth was able to respond to him.

"Of course your Majesty, I will organise a group to come with me, give me a day to make our plans. We will stamp this out and send a message to other villages, as you have asked," Beth replied.

The King dismissed his Knights. Beth headed straight to Alfred's chambers, where she knew that she would be uninterrupted and could safely contact Mother Nature. Once she was safe inside, she locked the door and took her own form again.

Beth immediately contacted Mother Nature and explained what was happening, she wanted permission to get involved and save the innocent people of the two villages.

"What would you propose we do Beth?" Mother Nature asked once she heard the plans.

"I know that each realm cannot know about another one, for their own safety and development, but we need to save these lives. Can we portal each village to another realm?" she asked.

"There are two that could take in some people, each has magic, we would be able to hide the new arrivals in their borders without too much trouble, how big are the villages?" she replied.

"They are small villages, each only has about four of five families, one of the families is Alfred's sister, her husband and children," she told Mother Nature.

"If we do this Beth, nobody can know where the villagers are, they must never find out that we have used magic to send them to other realms, Alfred must not know either."

Beth felt a huge knot in her stomach, Alfred would never know what happened to his sister, he may never see her again. She wondered if she could do that to him, but the alternative was that they could all die at the hands of the King and his Knights.

"Which realms can we use?" she asked.

"The two that I think would be best are Veridian and Ecurion, each has issues, but we could settle the villagers within them both. There is one other thing; the villagers must agree to this. We cannot force them to leave their homes, even if their lives are at risk."

"I will portal to Alfred's village first and talk to Helen, I am sure she will be able to persuade her neighbours that it will be best for them," Beth told Mother Nature.

Mother Nature agreed, she told Beth to let her know what the villagers decided. She urged her to move swiftly before the Knights had chance to get to them.

ALFRED'S STORY

As soon as she finished speaking to Mother Nature, Beth opened a portal to Alfred's home. In an instant she was stood at the door of their cabin, knocking on it loudly, hoping that they were in.

"Okay, I am coming," she heard shouting from inside.

When Helen opened the door, she found an agitated looking woman.

"Helen, my name is Beth, I am a friend of Alfred, can I come in?" she began.

Helen opened the door wider and let Beth in, she had not heard Alfred talk about her, but she thought that maybe she was a friend from the castle.

"How can I help you?" she asked.

Beth asked if she could sit down, then she began to explain who she was and why she was there. She told Helen of Alfred's quest to find his daughter and take her back to her son. Helen was shocked to find out that Alfred was the grandfather of the future King, and very proud too. She could not wait to meet her niece.

"I am stunned that Alfred is a father, I cannot wait to meet Dalfre," she told Beth.

Beth explained what the King was planning, she was apprehensive to tell her about never being able to see Alfred again, or ever meet his daughter, but she had to.

"Never? I will never see my brother again. How can you ask me to do that?" she asked.

"I am afraid you have a tough choice, it is simple, your brother or your husband and boys. The King will execute anyone he thinks is using magic. He thinks that your village is amongst those in rebellion against him. He has no idea that you are Alfred's sister. He will be safe in the castle, but you and your family cannot stay here. I am afraid we don't have much time. I need to get you and the others out of this realm and into another, where you can be safe," Beth told her.

Helen was amazed that there were other places apart from Dragoron. Magic was outlawed here, and Helen hadn't considered it possible that other places existed. Places where magic was practised freely ...

"Okay Beth, I understand the urgency. Let me gather the other families together and tell them what you have told me. They will have to make their own choices. I will also need to talk to my husband. Will you come with me?" she asked.

Beth said she would, and for the next couple of hours they spent their time travelling to each home through portals explaining what was happening to each family.

Beth left Helen to talk to her husband, she wasn't sure what they would decide, but eventually she had an answer from them all.

Luckily, with a lot of sacrifice each family decided that they would let Beth send them to another realm. She contacted Mother Nature and the evacuation of Alfred's village was soon underway, they were all being sent to Veridian.

The passage into Veridian had to be done quietly. There was an issue with the Queen of Veridian and so Mother Nature had decided that she would handle the relocation and settlement of the families herself. She opened the portal, and the families began to pass through.

Each of the refugee families stepped through the portal and into Veridian nervously; unsure of what this new life meant for them and what their futures would hold. Helen was the last through with her family. She asked Beth to tell Alfred goodbye and that she loved him very much, and that she hoped one day to see him again. Beth knew that for his own safety, Alfred could never receive that message.

Chapter 23

As soon as all the families were through the portal it closed behind them. Beth opened another one and was soon stood in the village where Farren and his family lived. She would have to start all over again and explain everything to another group.

The first thing she needed to do was to find the village elder Farren. It was market day, and the village was bustling. Although the village was small it had a very popular market that attracted many from the surrounding area. There were lots of people and Beth knew that this would take time, she thought she might have to wait until the market was finished.

"Hello," a young boy said to her.

"Hello young man, can you help me? I am looking for Farren, do you know where he is?" she asked.

"I can show you, but it will cost you the price of an apple," he said cheekily.

"It's a deal," she replied.

Both walked over to a stall in the market where Beth purchased an apple for the young boy, who took it, laughed and then ran off. Why had she been so trusting? He had cheek and mischief written all over him. She smiled to herself. Beth looked around and saw a tavern on the other side of the market square, she decided to try there.

When she opened the door and went in the tavern was empty, just a man sat by the fire with a tankard in his hand. Beth thought it a bit early for beer, but when she approached him she smelled the unmistakable smell of coffee, she hadn't smelled that since she had been in Dragoron and wondered where he had got it from.

"Good morning, sir. I am looking for Farren" she said to him "Do you know where I can find him?"

The man in the chair looked at her. His gaze making her feel uncomfortable, as if his eyes were exploring her soul. She broke his stare and looked around the room to see if anyone else could help.

"I am Farren," he said as she turned her back to him.

"I am a friend of Alfred, I have bad news for you and your villagers, would you be able to gather the families for a village meeting?" she asked.

"Why would I do that?" he asked, "Alfred has never mentioned you, you could be a spy from the King!"

Beth knew that this would be more difficult as soon as she arrived in the village, she had a feeling that she could not shake.

"May I sit?" she asked.

He nodded at her; she sat opposite him next to the fire. Beth began her tale, telling Farren exactly what was happening. He listened intently to her, he took in the plan to protect his friends and family. Mostly though he sat brooding. When she finished, he jumped up from his seat.

"Prove it!" he snapped.

"How exactly would you like me to do that?" she asked.

"Let me see your magic."

This demand didn't come as a surprise to Beth. She sat back in her chair with her eyes closed and focused her mind on Farren. Soon, she was in his thoughts, she had entered his mind. It was not something she would usually do, she firmly believed that the mind is the one place that a person should feel safe. Farren seemed steadfast in his mistrust of her and on this occasion, she needed something to convince him without doubt.

Beth began to trawl through his memories, showing Farren things that he had long forgotten. She then showed him some of her memories, specifically the meeting with the King. She could feel Farren's doubt begin to melt away, quickly being replaced by nervousness. Beth broke the link and opened her eyes, Farren's face was now ashen. She knew that he would agree to help her, now that he understood his family and friends were in danger.

"I will need some time, the market should be finished by early afternoon, everyone is here in the village today, so I can approach them all and arrange for a meeting. How will you persuade them?" he asked.

"You will be the one to give them the choice Farren. I can prove my magic if needed, but they will listen to you. You are the elder of the village," she told him.

"What is the realm like that we will go to? Will we be safe?" he asked.

"Mother Nature has chosen it; she says you will all be safe. I won't lie it will be difficult for you all to start with, but with you as their leader, your village should do well," Beth said reassuringly.

Farren told Beth that he would go and talk to the villagers about the meeting. He invited her to wait in the tavern and arranged for his wife to prepare her some food. Beth thanked him as he stood to leave.

Farren was gone for an hour or so. When he returned, he told her that the market was winding down, and people were leaving.

"The meeting will be here in about an hour, everyone has agreed to come. We total about 30. If everyone agrees, will we all be accommodated in the new realm?" he asked.

"Yes, you will, Mother Nature is aware of how many are in this village," she replied.

The next hour passed quickly, Beth answered as many of his questions as possible, but she could not answer them all. Thankfully when she got stuck Mother Nature appeared unexpectedly. Beth thought she would still be busy with Helen and her group in Veridian, but Mother Nature told her that they were all settled and that she had come to help this group. Farren could not believe his eyes. When Beth introduced them, he bowed down to her as if she was a queen.

"Please get up Farren, there is no need for that," she told him.

Mother Nature spent a little time reassuring Farren. By the time everyone arrived, he was clear about what he needed to tell them.

The meeting was relatively quiet, everyone was shocked by what had been said. All were completely unaware of any other realms and so they were understandably nervous about leaving their own homes. Farren told them what he saw and that he would protect them in their new homes. He did his best to assure them that they would be okay and safe. After quite a discussion, eventually they all agreed to leave and go to a place they had never heard of.

"I will open a portal to Ecurion" Mother Nature told them, "I will take you there now."

"But we need to gather our things together," someone shouted out.

"All you need will be provided for you, and I can magically arrange for your treasured possessions to arrive in your new homes," Mother Nature replied.

"Are you all ready?" she asked.

There was still some muttering and a lot of nervousness, but everyone said that they were. Mother Nature opened a portal. No one in the room had ever seen one before and some of the group jumped back in shock. It took some reassurance from Mother Nature, but they were soon convinced that it was safe for them to step through it to their new home.

One by one they went through until only Farren remained. He thanked Beth and stepped through.

"I have one question; how will you keep the realms secret now you have moved people between them?" Beth asked.

"I will enchant them. They will have memories, but they will be unable to tell anyone about Dragoron. This realm will be a foggy memory to them all, but still there in case one day those memories are needed," Mother Nature replied.

She told Beth to get back to the castle quickly and then stepped into the portal which closed behind her.

The next day the Knights, including Beth disguised as Trystrem, rode out to the two villages. They found only empty houses but that did not stop them destroying everything in sight. Leaving only burned-out buildings in the place of the villages. Beth was relieved that they had managed to save everyone, but she knew that in the process this would devastate Alfred.

Chapter 24

Dalfre, Alfred and Trystrem walked in silence. Each of them deep in thought about what they had discovered in the village. Dalfre was distraught that her uncle and his family had disappeared and so angry that someone had done that to the village. She knew who was responsible. She hoped that one day he would be brought to justice, but it was highly unlikely while he was the ruler of the realm.

Trystrem took her hand, he could sense the emotions coursing through her.

"We will find them Dalfre, I promise I will not stop searching," he told her.

Alfred was walking slightly in front of them both, his head bowed down. He didn't know what to say to Dalfre and he was worried about his sister and her family. He wasn't sure what he would do if anything happened to them. He hoped that their village was not attacked like Farren's had been.

The walk seemed endless to all three of them, none of them aware of their surroundings. The hours passed slowly, but eventually they were close to Alfred's home. Above the tree line thick black smoke could be seen rising into the sky and a loud crackling sound interrupted the silence. Alfred felt sick, he already knew that his family had been attacked, he knew that they were either gone, taken prisoner or dead. His heart broke before they even got to his home.

As they walked out of the woodlands, the sight in front of them was the same as at the previous village. There was nothing left except burning buildings, now almost completely burned to the ground. The fields of crops were just ash. There was nothing left, not one thing was salvageable from the fires. Alfred stopped in front of the last remnants of his home and fell to his knees, tears rolling down his cheeks.

His sobbing tore at the hearts of Dalfre and Trystrem. They both moved to kneel by his side, each of them with an arm around him to support him. Dalfre saw the life drain from Alfred, he seemed to age before her eyes.

"Why?" was all he could say.

Just as Trystrem was about to answer Alfred a portal opened behind them, Beth stepped out and immediately knelt by Alfred and embraced him.

"There was nothing I could do to stop the attacks Alfred, but I did manage to warn the villagers that the King wanted them destroyed. They had all gone by the time I arrived with the other Knights. Nobody was taken prisoner, and nobody was killed." She placed her hands on his face and looked him directly in his eyes "Alfred, they got away."

"Why this destruction, what was the point?" he replied.

"The King ordered it, I could only look on, I couldn't stop it," she told him.

"Do you know where everyone went?" he asked.

Beth knew that she could not tell him the truth. She said that she did not know. She told him that she had tried to find them, but they were so well hidden that she could not feel their presence.

"There must be a magical way to find them," he said.

"I have already checked, there isn't any way to find them if they want to stay hidden Alfred, I am so sorry," she lied.

Beth got to her feet and turned her attention to Dalfre and Trystrem.

"Dalfre, it is very nice to meet you, I am sorry that it is in these circumstances. The loss of your Uncle Farren and the family you knew there must be extremely hard, please let me know how I can help?" she said.

Dalfre didn't know what to say to Beth she just managed a thank you. She was so worried about her father that she had not processed the loss that she had suffered too. An aunt she would never know and an uncle she would never see again. She hoped that would not be the case but knew deep down it was unlikely that they would meet again.

"Trystrem, can I talk to you?" Beth asked.

Trystrem nodded, he kissed Dalfre on the cheek and left her with Alfred for a few moments while he talked to Beth.

"What are you plans? I see that Dalfre has changed in appearance from the woman I was introduced to."

"To Alfred and me, Dalfre looks the same. I am glad to know that to you she does not, it means the magic I gave up is protecting her, it means that we can get her into the castle," he replied.

"How are you planning that?" she asked.

"I will marry her, and introduce her to the King as my wife, in the hope that he will let her work in the castle near James."

"Dalfre is already married Trystrem, so that is not possible," she told him.

"But the King thinks that she is dead, he sees himself as a widower, so why can't I marry her? After all she is no longer Dalfre to anyone else," he replied.

Beth thought for a few moments, she couldn't answer that and told him that she would check with Mother Nature. If there was a way for them to marry, she would know.

"There is a lot to think about, Dalfre needs a new name, and you and Alfred will have to get used to calling her that. Any slip up would be catastrophic. If the King found out who she was and that she had used magic her life would end, he is a cruel and unforgiving man."

"I know, but we need to give them time to digest what has happened, don't we?"

"There is no time. I must leave here and return to my family. You all need to be back in the castle today."

Trystrem returned to Alfred and Dalfre. He told them about the discussion that the two of them had, both understood that they must return to the castle. Beth followed Trystrem back to the others a little while later after contacting Mother Nature.

"A new name, how do I choose that? I have always been Dalfre."

"Can I make a suggestion?" Alfred asked.

"Of course you can," she replied.

"Elena was your mother's second name; you could use that," Alfred suggested.

Dalfre loved the name, she told Alfred that she would be happy to keep a connection to her mother, so they all decided that Elena would be perfect.

"There is one other thing we need to do, Trystrem and I want to be married before we go to the castle, as I am no longer Dalfre then I consider the marriage to the King ended. Will you bless our union, Beth?" she asked.

"I cannot bless your union; I have asked Mother Nature if it is possible for you to marry Trystrem," she began.

"I will bless your union Elena and Trystrem," a voice answered from behind them all, Mother Nature was stood smiling at them.

"It is very unusual, but as Dalfre is dead and Elena is not married, I can see no reason why you should not marry. I must, however, make sure that you understand something: you must NEVER reveal your identity to anyone, especially not to James. If you do, many lives will be changed or lost forever. Your lives from today will be difficult but you must guide that young baby to adulthood. He must have a pure heart and be open to magic and only you can do that," she told them.

All three knew that it would be hard to keep their connection to James secret from him, but they all understood the implications if they didn't.

"Elena, Trystrem, please stand together in front of me," she said.

Mother Nature asked them both if they would love and protect each other, they replied that they would. She asked them to join hands and then announced that they were married and then she blessed their union by wishing them a safe and happy marriage. All of them knew that they would be together until the day they died.

"Beth and I must leave you now, but first we will get you back to the castle or close to it," she announced.

"How will I explain my absence from the castle?" Trystrem asked.

Beth told him that he had asked for a day away from the castle for a personal family reason, she told him that the King had given him to sunset that night to get back to his duties. Time enough for them to travel through a portal back to an area near the castle.

Beth opened a portal for the three of them. They each said their thanks and goodbyes before exhaustedly stepping through the portal and into the castle grounds.

Chapter 25

"I think it best that we don't all walk into the castle together, you two go on ahead and I will stay here and collect some herbs, nobody will think it odd when I walk back in with a handful of plants," he told Elena and Trystrem.

Elena hugged her father and told him that she would see him later, then both her and Trystrem walked towards the castle hand in hand. Alfred was happy that she had Trystrem to look after her too, he was a good man.

The walk to the castle was short, Trystrem told Elena that he would take her to his home and then go and see the King. He said that she should wait there while he tells the King of his marriage.

Trystrem lived in a small home within the castle walls. It had a room for eating, one for sleeping and one for bathing. It was clean and tidy, and when the fire was lit in the eating room it was warm and cosy, he hoped that Elena would be comfortable there. He was a little nervous, but as soon as he opened the door, and they went in her face lit up with a huge smile.

"What a wonderful home, it looks so cosy Trystrem, we will be happy here, it has everything we need," she told him after he had shown her the small rooms.

"I am glad you like it. It looks even cosier with the fire lit; I will light one for you before I go to the King," he replied.

Elena told him that he should go straight to the King, she said that she would light the fire, after all she had done it many times as a young girl, she hadn't always lived in a palace.

Trystrem kissed her on the cheek and left to see the King. He was nervous, he knew that he had broken the rules regarding marriage, he knew that he should have asked permission and that the King insisted on meeting future wives of the Knights. It was down to him whether they could marry. Trystrem had seen a few Knights refused permission, some gave up their place as a Knight, others gave up the dream of marriage with the woman they loved.

Stood in front of the large wooden door of the great hall, Trystrem took a deep breath and opened it. The King was sat with one of his advisors at the banquet table, they were deep in discussion and Trystrem waited by the door to be beckoned by the King.

Eventually the King looked at Trystrem and called him over, the advisor got up from the table and left the great hall. Trystrem took a deep breath and readied himself for a heated conversation with the King.

"Good evening Trystrem, did you sort out your family issues?" he asked.

"My Lord, I did thank you, but in the process, I broke your rules, I could not avoid it," he replied.

Trystrem looked directly at the King who already looked angry by what had been said, he told Trystrem to continue, he knew that he needed to tread carefully and had a story prepared.

"My family called me home because my mother was dying my Lord, it had always been her wish to see me married before she left. I could not refuse her dying wish, I know I should have introduced my Elena to you and asked for your permission, but I just did not have time, I am sorry," he lied.

The King looked at Trystrem intently, his icy stare piercing Trystrem's soul. Trystrem was scared, he knew that the King could banish him and Elena, he could imprison them if he chose. For a few minutes the King sat silently, mulling over his decision.

"Guards!!" he shouted.

Two guards entered the great hall immediately, the King asked Trystrem where Elena was, he told the King.

"Go and get the woman from Trystrem's house and bring her here immediately," he ordered the guards.

Trystrem's stomach turned, the King was angry, it worried him. He hoped that Elena would be okay, after all they had been through, he did not want things to go wrong now. The two men sat in silence and waited.

The doors opened to the great hall, the guards escorted Elena in, she stood in front of the King.

"You are Trystrem's wife?" he asked.

"I am my King," she replied.

"Do you know the rules of marriage for Knights?"

"No Sire, I am afraid I do not," Elena said.

The King explained that Trystrem had broken his rules by not asking permission or introducing Elena to him, he asked what she thought he should do about that as a punishment.

Elena knew what the rules were, she had been in the palace long enough as Dalfre to know that the King had complete control over his Knights, and that he would punish any of them severely if they broke his rules, but she had to play innocent and pretend that she did not.

"I am sorry Sire, I am sure whatever punishment you choose will be a fair one, one that we will abide by," she told him.

The King was a little taken aback by her response, he was used to people begging for mercy when they had crossed him, she puzzled him. He sat thinking, both Trystrem and Elena waited nervously for him to issue his decision.

"I do not agree with this marriage, you will both be..." the King began.

Suddenly as the King was talking the door flung open and a young woman ran in carrying a baby, Elena could see that it was James, her heart skipped a beat, he had grown so much in the time she had away.

"I am so sorry to interrupt my Lord, something is wrong with the Prince, he will not stop screaming, I have tried everything. I cannot find Alfred in case he is ill; I don't know what to do," she blurted out.

The King stood up from his seat and took his son from the maid. He sounded like he was in so much pain, but there was nothing obvious wrong with him. The screaming flustered the King, he shouted at the guards to find Alfred immediately.

"May I take him for you Sire?" Elena asked.

The King was never at ease with his son so handed him over to Elena, she took her son in her arms and began to sing a gentle lullaby to him, a lullaby only he had ever heard. One that she sang to him as a small baby when they were alone. James looked up at the woman holding him and stopped his screaming, he fell asleep in her arms. Elena knew their bond was still there, she looked at her son and her heart was full.

"How did you do that?" the King asked.

"I have always been good with children Sire; my mother called it a gift," she lied.

The King thought for a few moments, his anger with Trystrem slowly waning. He dismissed the maid and told her to leave the castle, she was no longer to look after the prince. She was visibly shocked but did as she was told, she knew better than to question the King.

"Ordinarily you and Trystrem would be severely punished for what you have done, but you have a way with my son. You will be his maid, his teacher and look after his every need," he told her.

Both Trystrem and Elena took deep breaths, they thanked the King for his leniency and Elena promised that she would take good care of the young prince.

"Trystrem, you will show your wife where the nursery is, show her around the castle, and you will prove your loyalty to me by NEVER breaking my rules again. I will not give you another chance, if you do then both of you will suffer greatly."

"Thank you, my Lord, I will not let you down again," he replied.

They both left the King in the great hall, Elena carried James to the nursery holding him close to her, she couldn't believe that they had managed it, it was as if James had sensed her in the castle. He had, even if he was too young to know it.

Chapter 26

Elena spent the evening bathing and settling James. Trystrem had left them alone together, he needed to arrange the training for the following day. He could not make a wrong move or upset the routine of the castle now, the King was watching them both closely. It would not take much for them to anger him again.

Before he did that though, Trystrem went to Alfred's chambers to let him know what had happened. Alfred was so happy that things had fallen into place so easily, he wondered if there had been any magical help from Beth.

The three of them met up at Trystrem's home once James was settled and fast asleep, each of them happy with the way things were going, they all hoped for a time of peace in the castle.

After they had chatted about the day, Alfred excused himself and left the newly married couple alone in their home and went back to his chambers. He knew that they needed time alone, a lot had happened to them both, their new life together had just begun.

When Alfred got back to his room, he looked in the mirror and called Beth, she answered him immediately.

"Alfred is everything okay?" she asked.

Alfred told her that everything was working out perfectly, he informed her that Elena had a job in the castle looking after James already, he did ask if any magic was involved in it at all? Beth did not answer, but she did give a knowing smile, he did not need to ask anymore.

"Thank you for everything Beth, I am so thankful that you came here, I owe you so much," he said.

"Alfred, it was my pleasure to help. Remember I will always be here when you need me, just as you are my eyes and ears when I am not around, we make a great team," she replied.

They chatted for a little while longer, then said goodbye to each other, for now.

The next few days in the castle were busy, Elena soon got into a routine with James, and both Trystrem and Alfred loved watching them together. Elena could make him laugh so easily; the baby prince was now a happy prince.

Trystrem settled back into his routine as the Knight in charge, luckily the King was not in a particularly bad mood, so there were no journeys beyond the castle walls to attack villages or hunt the dragons.

For a while it was peaceful. Alfred spent his time making potions to stock up his cupboards, mostly medicinal ones for the people of the realm when they were ill, but he also had many other potions hidden away for "just in case" scenarios.

The days soon turned into weeks, the weeks to months and all of them were comfortable with their new roles. Occasionally there was the odd slip up with Elena's name, but luckily nobody heard Alfred when he made those mistakes.

Alfred loved getting to know his daughter, she was a blessing to him and so was James, he knew that he would protect and be by his side whenever he needed him, as any grandfather would.

There were days that Alfred found difficult, he had been searching for news of Helen and her family as well as for news of Farren, but nobody could find out anything about where they were. It was as if they had disappeared into thin air, there was no sign of them at all. Alfred's heart was broken, and the only thing helping was spending time with Elena, Trystrem and James, the only family that he had left. Eventually he concluded that they must be dead, he gave up hope and spent most of his days in a deep grey mood, with no light or laughter.

On one sunny spring day Elena asked Alfred to accompany her and James on a walk and a picnic lunch, she knew that Alfred needed to leave the search behind, she would not watch him fall apart. She needed her father to be strong. After all, her time was limited with him, and she wanted to make each day count. Elena understood his heartbreak, she had lost Farren and his family too; but she knew that he would want her to live each day and be happy, that is what she needed to make Alfred understand.

Elena and Alfred walked through the flower meadows just outside the castle walls, Alfred carried James and Elena had a picnic basket. They talked about the weather, about what James had been doing, he had just taken his first steps and was into everything, he laughed constantly and was beginning to chatter to everyone he met, though it was mainly incomprehensible at that stage.

"Shall we sit here?" Elena asked when they got to the edge of the meadow at the start of the woodland.

"It is perfect," Alfred replied.

James was on the ground almost immediately, toddling around, sniffing the flowers. Elena put out a blanket and began to get the food out, it wasn't long before that caught the attention of the little prince, he loved eating!

The chat between father and daughter was light-hearted with James running around, but after he had eaten, he fell asleep on the blanket in the dappled sunshine.

"Father, we need to talk about Helen and Farren," Elena began, she could see Alfred tense up as soon as she started talking.

"I know Elena, just give me some more time," He replied.

"It has been months now, there is no news, we have to be realistic, they aren't coming back," she told him.

"I need you, so does Trystrem, you know that our time is limited here, I want every day to be special with you and James, so does Trystrem, there are days where we don't see you, you hide away from everyone."

"Please, can you tuck away your pain into a place in your heart? Can you make room for us? We are a family and one day it will just be you and James."

Alfred began to cry, he had not properly mourned the loss of his sister, his brother-in-law or nephews before, he had been busy searching for them and had not fully accepted that they were not coming back. When Elena began to talk to him the grim reality finally hit him, this time harder than the day they discovered the village destroyed. The tears tumbled down his cheeks, he fell into the arms of his daughter, she held him tight as he sobbed and sobbed, his whole body wracked with the force of his grief. Elena's heart broke for him, she had never seen anyone so upset, so fragile.

When the tears and sobbing eventually stopped Elena sensed that a weight had lifted from her father, she looked deep into his eyes and saw the pain, but it was not as obvious as it had been, there was a clarity in them, and maybe even some peace.

Alfred felt his heart beating again, it had been so heavy since that day, he was grateful that Elena had forced him to face reality. She was right, her time was limited, he wanted to make sure that she had a happy life, he wanted to spend as much time as he could with her.

"Thank you," he said, "I love you Elena, I needed you to make me see."

Chapter 27

Almost twenty years later

A happy life is exactly what Elena, Trystrem, Alfred and James had. James grew into a strong man, a happy, kind and compassionate one. All three were proud of him.

Even through dark days when the King was rampaging, Trystrem was able to warn villages and the Dragons of any impeding danger. Mostly he succeeded, but unfortunately not all the time. There were deaths and there were prisoners taken. James saw the consequences of crossing his father and he learned early on to keep his opinions secret, but he knew one day that the realm would be a much safer place.

The months and years flew by. Knowing that Elena and Trystrem would be gone very soon, they spent as much time as possible with James. Trystrem trained him in swordsmanship, Elena guided him on how to treat people, how to show compassion and when the time for them to leave drew close, they both knew that he would be a great King. They knew that they had done what was needed.

Elena and Trystrem were each dreading that day, neither wanted to leave Alfred or James. Their hearts grew heavier as they got closer to the time that they had to go.

"Alfred, you know that we only have a few days left, don't you?" Trystrem asked him over dinner one evening.

"I do, it is a time I have been dreading since the day we found out. I don't know how I am going to say goodbye to you both," he replied.

"Elena and I have been talking, we will have to travel back to the cave of the first magical dragon before we die, will you come with us? Will you be by our side when the time comes?" he asked.

Alfred had not thought about where it would happen or how. He did not want to face it, but now he could not avoid it. His beloved daughter and son-in-law needed him, but he knew that he could not be with them when it happened, all he could do was to be with them for as long as he could.

"Of course I will come with you both, I am honoured to be by your sides, you are my family and I love you both very much," he replied.

"We need to leave tomorrow night, I have sent word to Agra to meet us outside the borders of the castle, he will take us back, and like you he will be with us at the end."

Alfred could see tears welling in Elena's eyes, he knew that she would be saying goodbye to her son the following day, it was going to be the most difficult day for her. He also knew that James must not think that anything was different, he could not ever know who she was.

Alfred left them both, they needed time together in their own home to prepare for what was to come, he hated leaving them. Trystrem and Elena spent the remainder of the evening reminiscing about their time with James, laughing and crying about all the milestones, the first words, the first steps, the first time he disarmed Trystrem of his sword and the first time he smiled at them both, there were endless good times to talk about, both avoiding the fact that there would be no more.

The night passed, sleep was short, neither of them wanting to waste a moment. The following morning they each went to their usual parts of the castle, Elena to James and Trystrem to the Knights quarters. The day passed too quickly. It was a blur but each of them subtly said goodbye to James and to the other important people that they had grown to love.

Just as the sun was going down all three met at the edge of the meadow. Elena and Trystrem took one last look back at the place that had been a happy home for them for almost twenty years.

The walk through the meadow and woodlands was silent, each one of them deep in thought, each heart slowly breaking as they walked closer to the place where they were meeting Agra.

Alfred held Elena's hand never wanting to let it go. He knew that he could not hold it for much longer, the grief he felt when he lost his sister was rising in his body again, his heart growing heavy in his chest. Elena squeezed his hand; she knew what he was feeling and cuddled into her father as they walked.

It wasn't long before they were stood waiting for Agra, and moments after they arrived he landed in front of them. He bowed his head to Trystrem.

"My Lord, this is a sad time for us all," he said.

"We will fly to where we stopped last time and then continue on tomorrow to the cave, we will arrive by the afternoon of our final day," Trystrem said.

Agra, Alfred and Elena nodded, nobody had anything they could say. Each were swallowing their feelings; trying to put on brave faces for the others and failing miserably.

"Climb on," Agra said as he bowed down low enough for them to.

Moments later they were flying away towards their destiny, towards their impending death. The heavens opened, the sky was crying the tears that they were all trying to hide, each openly joining in.

A few hours later Agra landed in the familiar spot, it had been many years, but it was just the same as it was almost twenty years ago.

"We will rest here tonight, tomorrow we fly the rest of the way," Trystrem reminded them.

Sleep eluded them all that night, there was the odd conversation, but mostly each sat in silence lost in their own thoughts. Elena wondered what it would be like to die, she hoped it would be painless and like she was falling asleep. Alfred replayed memories of his time with Elena and Trystrem through his mind, it bought him comfort.

The sun rose too soon for them all, they were soon soaring through the sun filled sky on a beautiful day towards the cave of the first magical dragon, towards a destiny that neither Elena nor Trystrem could avoid.

Agra landed in front of the snow topped mountain, the cave entrance hidden by greenery, nobody could have guessed what was behind it.

"Agra, this time you and Alfred will be able to come in with us, there is no test, just a time to say goodbye to those we love. Will you do that for us?" Trystrem asked, choking back his emotions.

"I would be honoured my Lord Tora," he replied, equally as upset.

As soon as Agra replied the greenery fell away and a familiar thundering sound followed by falling rocks began. In no time at all the large cave entrance was in view.

"Are you ready?" Trystrem asked Elena.

"Yes," she replied.

Chapter 28

The four of them walked into the cave. Ahead they could see the orb sat on the rock altar, the same purple glow emanating from it.

"Welcome Elena and Trystrem, I hope you have lived a happy life and guided the young prince well?" Adrianna asked.

"James is a kind and compassionate man, when he becomes King, he will be a great one," Trystrem replied.

"Alfred, Agra it is nice to meet you, I am sorry that it is a sad occasion for you both, but know it was the only way" she said.

"How do we die?" Elena asked, "Will it hurt?"

"Elena, I can promise you, there will be no pain, it will be peaceful" she replied, "Please say your goodbyes, we will begin immediately."

Both Elena and Trystrem hugged Alfred and Agra, all were battling tears, but somehow, they managed to say the final words that they wanted to. Alfred told them he would love them always, he told them he was proud of them both and he promised to stay by James' side, no matter what.

"Please come here and lie in front of the altar," they were told.

There was a soft bed in front of the altar, it felt like they were just going to rest, there were big pillows for them to rest their heads on. Alfred and Agra watched as they both lay down next to each other, holding hands and looking extremely nervous. Elena looked over at Alfred. Her eyes filled with tears and her smile fixed and unconvincing. Alfred smiled back, trying to reassure her, then she turned her head to her husband, both had their eyes fixed on each other.

"I love you Trystrem, I always will," Elena told the man who held her heart.

"I love you too, may we meet again one day my love," he replied.

Alfred's heart broke in two, how could he stand there and watch them die, how could he lose them? He closed his eyes, fighting back the grief. He was trying to stay strong, but he couldn't stop the tears.

"It is time," Adrianna told them "Welcome home Tora," she continued.

As soon as she said that a purple light radiated from the orb, it gently made its way towards Elena and Trystrem, slowly and softly moving through the darkness of the cave, the light broke into two, one of them floating towards Elena and the other one towards Trystrem, they closed their eyes and squeezed each other's hand tight, scared of what was coming.

The gentle light touched each of them on the top of their heads, it felt like a kiss to them both. The instant that it touched them, they both relaxed. All fear had evaporated, and a calmness engulfed them. They opened their eyes and looked at each other, both at peace, both ready for death.

Agra and Alfred looked on, they could see the peace in Elena and Trystrem, they too felt the calmness in the cave.

Moments later the light surrounded both Elena and Trystrem, lifting them both off the ground and into the air. The light swirled around them until Agra and Alfred could no longer see them. Round and round it went, growing brighter each moment. Eventually it returned to the ground.

Agra and Alfred could not believe what they were seeing, it was truly a sight to behold.

As the light retreated to the orb it revealed two dragons laying on the ground, Trystrem was back in his true form, but Elena was also in the form of a dragon. They opened their eyes, both not sure what had just happened.

"Tora you are restored to your form ready to take your final journey home," Adrianna said.

Everyone was confused why Elena was in dragon form, but they were about to find out why.

"Elena, you are now Dalfre, you are in the form ready for your final journey, it has been decided because of your sacrifice and your heart, the heart of a dragon, you will not be separated from Tora, you will be together for eternity," she began.

"You gave up your chance to have a child together, with your sacrifice the next magical dragon will be born, you together will give the world that," she continued.

Both Dalfre and Tora were confused, they were expecting death, now they were being told that they would produce the next magical dragon.

"Please say a final goodbye," she told them.

"I love you Dad," Dalfre shouted to her father.

Moments later the light reappeared, it again lifted Dalfre and Tora gently from the ground, it engulfed them again, this time swirling around them both, getting tighter and tighter around them, before the eyes of Alfred and Agra, the light got smaller and smaller, brighter and brighter. They could barely look at it anymore as it was so bright that it was blinding.

Suddenly the cave went black. No light could be seen at all. Alfred and Agra did not know what to do, they waited to see if anything else happened, unable to move from where they stood, both still shocked at the sight of Dalfre as a dragon.

After a few moments, the orb lit back up and in front of the altar was a large pale purple egg, a dragon egg.

"Agra, Alfred, this is Kayda, this egg will hatch into the next magical dragon, she was born from the love of Dalfre and Tora, she will be a great dragon," Adrianna told them both.

"Where are Dalfre and Tora?" Agra asked.

"Because of their love and dedication to each other, and the way they have guided the young prince, their souls have joined us here. They have joined the souls of the previous magical dragons; they will live on in us and will never be parted," she told them.

"Will we ever be able to see them again?" Alfred asked.

"I am afraid not, just know that they will always be a part of each other, they will never know pain or distress, just peace," she told them.

"What about the egg, who will look after it until it hatches? Who will raise the dragon?" Agra asked.

"Kayda will be raised by us here, the spirits of the magical dragons, including Tora and Dalfre, it has been done before, Tora was raised here too," she replied.

"It is time for you to go now, as soon as you leave the cave you will not remember what you have seen here, you will remember that you had a daughter once that you longed to meet, and you will remember Elena, but you will not be able to connect the two. You will have fond memories of Elena and Trystrem. If anyone asks you where they are, you will not know," she told them.

ALFRED'S STORY

Moments later Agra and Alfred were standing outside the hidden cave, both wondering what they were doing there, both aware of a loss but confused as to why they were where they were.

Agra flew Alfred back to the woodlands near the castle, they flew in silence, neither knew what to say.

Once Agra landed, they both said goodbye, each telling the other that they were there if they were needed.

Alfred walked into the castle, back to his chamber.

Chapter 29

Not long after he got back into his room, there was a knock on the door, he opened it to find Prince James stood there.

"Sire, how can I help you, are you ill?" Alfred asked.

"No Alfred, I am quite well, I was wondering if you had seen Elena, and my father is looking for Trystrem, do you have any idea where they might be?"

Alfred felt that he knew something, but he couldn't quite recall what. He did not remember Elena as his daughter, she was the maid that looked after James. He wanted to tell James that they were both dead for some reason, but he hesitated.

"I don't know where they are, I can ask around and see if anyone knows," he replied.

"Thank you, I will leave it with you, come and see me once you find out, they seem to have disappeared into thin air."

Alfred looked at the prince, he felt a presence in him, he hoped it was his daughter's spirit, he also felt extreme love for his grandson. Alfred hoped that Dalfre had not suffered when the King had her killed. It was a blessing that James had never found out about the way the King treated her and that he believed that she died not long after he was born. It haunted Alfred that he never got to meet her; he was consoled by the thought that she would have loved James greatly.

Alfred spent the afternoon pottering in his rooms, making some medicines, he had a nagging feeling that he could not pinpoint. After supper he went to bed.

A couple of hours into his sleep, he began to dream, he dreamt of Elena and Trystrem, they were in the mountains, happy and in love, they always made him feel contented when he saw them together like that. Alfred looked on in his dream as they walked, talked and laughed together, he was smiling in his sleep watching them.

Suddenly Trystrem drew his sword, a gang of men had surrounded them both, they were shouting at them both to kneel. Trystrem did not and told Elena not to either. They both stood their ground, the men charged at them both with swords drawn, Trystrem tried his best to protect his wife, but there were too many, Alfred was looking on at their lifeless bodies on the rocks, he woke up in tears and wondered if what he had seen was just a dream, he hoped that it wasn't true that his friends were dead. He had a feeling that they were. What Alfred did not know was that the dream had been planted in his memories by Adrianna.

First thing in the morning he was up and asking everyone who worked in the castle if they had seen them both, nobody had, one maid thought that she saw them leaving the castle early one morning together, but she couldn't be sure. Alfred went to see Prince James; he was in the great hall with the King.

Alfred bowed in front of them both and asked them to excuse his interruption.

"Prince James, I have asked around nobody is sure where Elena or Trystrem are, one maid thinks she saw them leaving the castle, but she couldn't swear to it," he told him.

"Does she know where they might have gone?" he asked Alfred.

"No Sire, but they do like to spend time in the mountains together," he told them.

"There have been attacks in the mountains recently, we have had reports of men robbing people on their journeys through them," the King announced.

"Trystrem is an excellent swordsman, he would be able to deal with a few untrained men. They should be back by now," Prince James replied.

"Send some Knights out to check," he was told.

Prince James called the Knights and asked them to head into the mountains to see if he could find them both. The Knights left immediately. Alfred worried about his friends and eagerly waited for the Knights to return, he spent the day in his chambers, he didn't do anything, he just sat and waited.

The Knights did not return that night, they were away from the castle for another couple of days searching for Elena and Trystrem, Alfred was unnerved, he was worried about his friends and had an ominous feeling that his dream may be true. Eventually they returned, but Elena and Trystrem were nowhere to be seen. The Knights explained to the King and Prince James that they had searched the mountains and couldn't fine either of them, they did say that they had found an area that had signs of a fight, they told the King that there was blood, but no bodies. So it was assumed that Elena and Trystrem were both dead. Alfred was heartbroken, they had been close friends for many years, he knew how much Prince James had depended on them both for support, he never got that from the King.

Over the next few days, with no news on Elena and Trystrem to contradict the thought of them both dying, Prince James arranged for a service for them both, he knew that many would want to say goodbye to the couple, many loved them in the castle. It was a hard day and full of many tears from all who knew them, Alfred cried so much, he was going to miss his friends.

Life moved on in the castle, Beth spent time with Alfred from time to time, she became a close friend and somebody he was quite enchanted with.

The days rolled into months, the months into years and one day the King became ill. He had waged war on magic and his people for so long, nobody was upset when he succumbed to his illness and died, in fact there was relief and joy on the day that Prince James became King James.

The first thing the new King did was to decree that the dragons would now be protected and anyone who hurt or killed one would be dealt with severely, Alfred knew he would be a great King.

Alfred never remembered what he saw in the cave, he never remembered spending time with Dalfre before she became Elena. He took solace in his relationship with King James, a friendship that would last many, many years.

Epilogue

Alfred became the sole protector of Dragoron when Beth died unexpectedly, for many years he kept Mother Nature informed of any issues, but there were not many to report.

Dragoron was a peaceful and happy realm, until one day when...

Find out more in Lottie Jones and the Magical Realms: Dragoron the first in the fantasy fiction series following the new High Sorceress and Protector of the Magical Realms.

About the Author

HS Matthews is a writer of Children and Teen Fantasy Fiction novels, her debut novel Lottie Jones and The Magical Realms, Dragoron is the first in a series of books following Lottie Jones from her life as an ordinary young girl to a life quite extraordinary, full of magic, sorcery and adventure!

Currently there are three titles available in the series, they are Dragoron, Veridian and newly released Calithia.

HS Matthews lives in Southern England with her husband and dogs, two wonderful spaniels who are full of energy! When not writing or working at her day job as an accountant HS, her husband and dogs love nothing more than exploring the local countryside on long walks, whether in the rain or the sunshine.

HS Matthews has two children and two grandchildren, inspired by her love of reading fantasy fiction books she has written stories that her grandchildren love to read.

Currently working on the final instalment of the Lottie Jones series, HS is constantly busy but loves the challenges of fitting her writing into her busy schedule.

A message from the Author

Thank you for reading Alfred, he is a huge character in the Lottie Jones and the Magical Realms series, and I have loved writing his story for you.

If you loved reading about Alfred be sure to check out the first book in the Lottie Jones series Dragoron to see what more adventures there are in store for him.

Enjoy the adventures and if you have, don't forget to leave a review so that others can discover the story you have enjoyed.

Best wishes

H S Matthews

Acknowledgement

A special thank you to Jaime Ricciardi for the beautiful image on the cover, you captured my vision perfectly.